Brexit

Other Books of Related Interest

At Issue Series

Assimilation
Does the World Hate the United States?
Immigration Reform
Should the US Close Its Borders?

Current Controversies Series

Islamophobia
Politics and Religion
The World Economy

Opposing Viewpoints Series

America's Global Influence
Democracy
The European Union
Illegal Immigration

Viewpoints on
Modern World History

Brexit

Caleb Bissinger, Book Editor

GREENHAVEN
PUBLISHING

Published in 2018 by Greenhaven Publishing, LLC
353 3rd Avenue, Suite 255, New York, NY 10010

First Edition

Articles in Greenhaven Publishing anthologies are often edited for length to meet page requirements. In addition, original titles of these works are changed to clearly present the main thesis and to explicitly indicate the author's opinion. Every effort is made to ensure that Greenhaven Publishing accurately reflects the original intent of the authors. Every effort has been made to trace the owners of the copyrighted material.

Cover image: lazyllama/Shutterstock.com

Library of Congress Cataloging-in-Publication Data

Names: Bissinger, Caleb, editor.
Title: Brexit / Caleb Bissinger, book editor.
Description: New York : Greenhaven Publishing, [2018] | Series: Viewpoints on modern world history | Includes bibliographical references and index. | Audience: Grades 9-12.
Identifiers: LCCN 2017030105 | ISBN 9781534501416 (library bound)
Subjects: LCSH: European Union--Great Britain--Juvenile literature. | Referendum--Great Britain--Juvenile literature. | Great Britain--Politics and government--2007-
Classification: LCC JF497.G7 B7598 2018 | DDC 341.242/230941--dc23
LC record available at https://lccn.loc.gov/2017030105

Manufactured in the United States of America

Website: http://greenhavenpublishing.com

Contents

Chapter 2: Perspectives, Controversies, and Debates

Chapter 3: What's Next for the UK, the EU, and the World?

Foreword

"The more we know about the past enables us to ask richer and more provocative questions about who we are today. We also must tell the next generation one of the great truths of history: that no past event was preordained. Every battle, every election, and revolution could have turned out differently at any point along the way, just as a person's own life can change unpredictably."

—David McCullough, American historian

History is punctuated by momentous events—turning points for the nations involved, with impacts felt far beyond their borders. Displaying the full range of human capabilities—from violence, greed, and ignorance to heroism, courage, and strength—they are nearly always complicated and multifaceted. Any student of history faces the challenge of grasping both the broader elements and the nuances of world-changing events, such as wars, social movements, and environmental disasters. Textbooks offer only so much help, burdened as they are by constraints of length and single-perspective narratives. True understanding of history's significant events comes from exposure to a variety of perspectives from the people involved intimately, as well as those observing from a distance of miles or years.

Viewpoints on Modern World History examines global events from the twentieth century onward, presenting analysis and observation from numerous vantage points. The series offers high school, early college level, and general interest readers a thematically arranged anthology of previously published materials that address a major historical event or period. Each volume opens with background information on the event, presents the controversies surrounding the event, and concludes with the implications and legacy of the event. By providing a variety of perspectives, this series can be used to inform debate, help develop critical thinking skills, increase global awareness, and enhance an understanding of international viewpoints on history.

Material in each volume is selected from a diverse range of sources. Articles taken from these sources are carefully edited and introduced to provide context and background.

Each volume in the Viewpoints on Modern World History series also includes:

- An annotated **table of contents** that provides a brief summary of each essay in the volume
- An **introduction** specific to the volume topic
- A **chapter preface** setting up the chapter content and providing historical context
- For each viewpoint, a brief **introduction** that has notes about the author and source of the viewpoint and provides a summary of its main points
- Informational **sidebars** that explore the lives of key individuals, give background on historical events, or explain scientific or technical concepts
- A **chronology** of dates important to the period
- A **bibliography** of additional books, periodicals, and websites for further research
- A **subject index** that offers links to people, places, and events cited in the text

Viewpoints on Modern World History is designed for a broad spectrum of readers who want to learn more about not only history but also current events, political science, government, international relations, and sociology. This includes students doing research for class assignments or debates, teachers and faculty seeking to supplement course materials, and others wanting to improve their understanding of history. The volumes in this series are designed to illuminate a complicated event, to spark debate, and to show the human perspective behind the world's most significant happenings of recent decades.

Introduction

If Britain must choose between Europe and the open sea, she must always choose the open sea.

— Winston Churchill

In March 1957, representatives from six nations—Belgium, France, Italy, Luxembourg, the Netherlands, and West Germany—gathered in Rome at the peach-colored Palazo dei Conservatori, which was designed by Michelangelo, and formed the European Economic Community (EEC), the precursor to today's European Union. The goal of the EEC was to let goods and people cross borders without cost or imposition. (Today, the EU is centered around the common market, which refers to the free movement of goods, people, capital, and services.) Nearly two decades later, in 1973, the United Kingdom—and its constituent parts: England, Wales, Scotland, and Northern Ireland—signed on. Edward Heath, who was then Prime Minister, said: "We will find there is a great cross-fertilisation of knowledge and information, not only in business but in every other sphere. And this will enable us to be more efficient and more competitive in gaining more markets not only in Europe but in the rest of the world."

Now, 40 years and a hair later, after a rattling referendum—the Brexit vote—that shocked the status quo and set in motion the UK's separation from the EU, that cross-fertilization has gone to seed.

In the following pages, you'll encounter viewpoints that show you Brexit from all sides—its domestic causes and its global ramifications, its xenophobic rallying call and its false promises, its historical precedent and its certain uncertainty. First, though, a little background.

In January, 2013, Prime Minister David Cameron, under pressure from members of his own party (the Conservatives), and the increasingly vociferous UK Independence Party (UKIP), announced that, so long as he kept his post, the citizens of the United Kingdom would, in three years' time, vote on the UK's continued membership in the European Union. To bear the cost of cost or revel in the triumph; are we in or are we out?

Thus began the battle of Brexit. On one side, you had the Remain campaign; led by Cameron, it advocated for the UK's continued membership in the EU—albeit with a set of reforms aimed at curbing immigration and giving the UK additional autonomy—citing the financial disaster that exiting would entail. Imagine a less competitive UK, they told voters, where fewer and fewer business are keen to set up shop, and add to it a £20 billion divorce settlement with the EU. On the other side, you had the pro-Brexit Leavers led by Boris Johnson, London's mayor; Lord Chancellor Michael Gove of the Conservative Party; and Nigel Farage, leader of the UK Independence Party. Their demands were simple, their grievances long. They were fed up with what they saw as the profane power of an undemocratic institution. (It's worth pointing out here that, while the members of the European Commission are appointed and charged with drafting laws, those laws are voted on by the publically elected European Parliament.) In an appeal to the working class, the Leave campaign bemoaned the rise of immigration and job insecurity. They also dispensed a ton of misinformation. They falsely stated that the UK sends £350 million a week to the EU; made the specious, racist claim that Turkey would soon join the EU and its citizens would flock to England to live and commit crimes; and, when faced with legitimate objections to their trickery, defended themselves simply by expressing their exhaustion with experts. Whenever they could, they turned the conversation to migration, which is why many observers now point to May 26, 2016, as a decisive day in the Brexit battle, for that was when the Office for National Statistics announced that net migration in 2015 was 330,000—"a record number of people came to the UK to find work."

The referendum vote was held on June 23, 2016. Leave won 52% to 48%. David Cameron resigned the next day, and Theresa May succeeded him. Now that Brexit was indeed to be the nation's fate, a great debate emerged as to what exactly that meant. Would it be a "soft Brexit," wherein the UK's exit from the EU would be more of a gesture than anything else and Britain would maintain access to the common market? (The EU, for its part, was not hot on this idea; it was eager to penalize the UK to stop other nations from following Britain's lead.) Or would it be a "hard Brexit," wherein the UK would abandon the common market altogether?

Hard Brexit won out. In early 2017, Theresa May outlined her government's Brexit strategy. The UK, she said, would indeed quit the common market, and she would soon trigger Article 50, the formal mechanism whereby a member state leaves the EU. Then in November the High Court ruled that tripping Article 50 required an act of Parliament. Some saw a last-ditch opportunity to annul Brexit, but, in the end, Parliament respected the referendum vote, and the act approving Article 50 came through in March 2017.

Finally, in June 2017, May called a snap election. She wanted to show that she and the Conservative Party had strong public support for their Brexit strategy. The plan backfired, and the Conservatives lost their parliamentary majority.

Now, a great many details are left to be worked out—not the least of which is the question of what sort of trade deals will the UK secure. It could be a decade before we have a complete answer. And then there's the question of motive. As Zadie Smith observed in an essay written after the referendum vote, it's next to impossible to boil Brexit down to a single issue. "What was it really about?" she asked. "Immigration? Inequality? Historic xenophobia? Sovereignty? EU bureaucracy? Anti-neoliberal revolution? Class war? … One useful consequence of Brexit is to finally and openly reveal a deep fracture in British society that has been thirty years in the making. The gaps between north and south, between the social classes, between Londoners and everyone else, between rich Londoners and poor Londoners, and between white and brown and black are real and need to be confronted by all of us."

As you read on in *Viewpoints on Modern History: Brexit*, you'll be confronting those gaps, too.

Chapter 1

The Path to Brexit

Preface

We humans, we students of history, have a robust predilection for squeezing catalyzing incidents out of mishmash. We seek the face that launched a thousand ships. We know that Rome was founded on April 21, 753 BCE, because that's the date Romulus slew his brother Remus. World War I, we say with reductive certainty, began on June 28, 1914, with the assassination of Archduke Franz Ferdinand. We call such moments, moments that send civilization bounding in a new direction, epochs.

There is a tendency, when looking back on Brexit, to do something similar. Surely the raison d'être is buried in England's decades-long colonial enterprise. Or perhaps it has something to do with the United Kingdom's "special relationship" with the United States. No, you know what? Brexit was the explosion of the UK's long-simmering racial animus, and white men scrambled to safeguard their hegemonic masculinity. None of these explanations are wrong, of course, but none of them are quite right either—or at least quite right on their own. Xenophobia, populism, misfortune, stagnation, hubris, and treachery all together ushered in the Brexit epoch. And the viewpoints in this chapter chart the rounded lineup of Brexit's instigators so that you may come away with a clear sense of the intricate factors at work.

"Scrutiny of a minute section of time and space," John Updike wrote, "[yields] strangenesses—gaps, inconsistencies, warps, and bubbles in the surface of circumstance." This chapter closes those gaps so that economic unease and social shortcomings draw together. The writers you'll meet in the next few pages are economists, academics, and journalists. Each is thoughtful and each makes a compelling case for their diagnosis of what provoked Brexit.

Viewpoint 1

Brexit Is About History

James Dennison and Noah Carl

Xenophobia, austerity, and dissatisfaction with politics may have contributed to the Brexit vote. But author James Dennison and editor Noah Carl write that, although a number of concerns may have tipped the balance, Brexit was ultimately decided by more than recent events. Here, the academic researchers demonstrate how the UK has been the least well-integrated EU member state, and so the closer the EU was moving toward political union, the more likely Brexit was becoming.

Since the British electorate voted to leave the European Union, many commentators have sought to explain (and often decry) the referendum's outcome as the result of a misleading and demagogic Leave campaign, irrational xenophobia, simple racism, an obstinate protest vote, the government's fiscal austerity policies, a largely Eurosceptic press, or general discontent about the economy. While several of these explanations have at least some merit, we believe they are insufficient. Indeed, they either put too much emphasis on recent events, or mistakenly assume that few Leave voters were motivated by dissatisfaction with Britain's EU membership *per se*.

Regarding the former, a recent analysis of internet and phone polls suggests that Leave may actually have had the lead throughout the entire campaign, belying the claim that provocative statements made by Nigel Farage or Boris Johnson exerted decisive sway

---

"The ultimate causes of Brexit: history, culture, and geography," by James Dennison and Noah Carl, London School of Economics, July 18, 2016. Reprinted by Permission.

over prospective voters. Regarding the latter, evidence from the BES internet panel and Lord Ashcroft's large post-referendum poll suggests that overall national sovereignty may have been just as important an issue for Leavers as immigration, and that austerity hardly registered.

Opposition to Britain's membership of the EU has fluctuated over the years, but has remained substantial ever since the UK joined in the mid 1970s; somewhere between ~30 and ~60 per cent of the British public has always been opposed to EU membership. Of course, the Eurosceptic fraction of the population almost certainly increased as a consequence of the rapid rise in EU immigration, which began in the late 1990s, and the Eurozone debt crises, which precipitated mass unemployment across Southern Europe. Nevertheless, the most important phenomenon to be explained vis-à-vis the referendum result in our view is that a sizable Eurosceptic faction has remained extant in Britain over the last four decades, in contrast to the other countries of Europe.

In *The American Voter*, one of the seminal studies on voting behaviour, Angus Campbell arranged the myriad factors affecting vote choice within a so-called funnel of causality: ultimate causes—such as structural and historical factors—were placed on the left hand side of the diagram, while proximate causes—such as attitudes to individual policies and candidates—were placed on the right hand side. Similarly, and we show that in a number of important respects, the UK is the least well-integrated EU member state—essentially, the least European country—and that this fact likely stems from certain historical features, which arguably constitute the ultimate causes of Brexit.

The UK is ranked 28 out of 28 for European identity: nearly two-thirds of Britons do not identify as European at all, compared to fewer than 40 per cent of French and Italians, and fewer than 30 per cent of Spanish and Germans.

The UK is ranked 26 out of 28 [for trust in the European Union]: fewer than 30 per cent of Britons trust the EU, compared to 39 per cent of Germans, 47 per cent of Dutch and a full 57 per cent of Danes.

[...]

The UK's comparatively limited integration into the EU is manifested in citizens' self-identity, in their mistrust of the EU, in patterns of emigration, in international trade flows, and in foreign investment allocations. While the UK is not the lowest-ranked country on every single measure, it consistently ranks among the bottom two or three; the only countries that come close are Greece and Cyprus —both of which have suffered financial crises in recent years.

Britons' comparatively less European self-identity and lower trust in the EU may have come about for the following reasons. First, Britain is the only allied European power not to have been occupied during the Second World War. Second, Britain has its own common law legal system, which contrasts with the civil law system of continental Europe. Third, because Britain has an established church, most British Christians have historically owed their allegiance to a national institution headed by the monarch, rather than to an international institution headed by the Pope. Fourth, Britain is an island whose surrounding waters have partially isolated it from cultural developments on the continent.

The fact that Britain does relatively more of its trade and investment outside of the EU, is due at least partly to the size and economic development of its former empire, the status of English as the global business language, and its particularly close ties with the United States.

All of these factors have served to stymie over-enthusiastically pro-EU business policy, exemplified most clearly in the previous Labour government's decision to not join the Euro. In addition, Britain's colonial past surely explains why relatively fewer of its emigrants choose to resettle in the EU. Indeed, several former British territories today have large British-descended populations.

In conclusion, Britain is the least well-integrated EU member state: European, just not European enough. While short-term contingencies and concerns about other issues may have tipped the balance toward Leave, as the EU moved closer toward political union, the UK's fundamentally less European character meant that Brexit was increasingly likely.

Viewpoint 2

Where Do We Go from Here?

Lionel Barber

In the following viewpoint, Financial Times *editor Lionel Barber, plots a cogent history of Britain's relationship with Europe since World War II. "Unlike the French and the Germans," he writes, "scarred by three wars inside a century, we [the English] always saw Europe as an economic transaction rather than a political project." So why vote to change things? Barber believes the voters—enough of them, anyway—were troubled by the imbalance of "supranational powers" against "loose intergovernmental co-operation;" afraid of catching the EU's high-unemployment, low-growth bug; tired of the establishment; and frightened by the "twin crises" of immigration and terrorism.*

In the early hours of June 24, the British people woke up to a revolution. There was no storming of Buckingham Palace or Downing Street. But the referendum vote in favour of Brexit was a popular revolt, a gut-wrenching defeat for the "establishment." The UK government, the Bank of England, the International Monetary Fund, the OECD, a number of world leaders including President Barack Obama of the US and Prime Minister Shinzo Abe of Japan and, yes, the Financial Times, all argued that a vote to leave the EU made no economic sense. We lost. They won.

They, the Brexiters, now face any number of awkward questions. What will Britain's future relationship be with the EU? What will

---

"Britain after Brexit: Lionel Barber's lecture in Tokyo," by Lionel Barber, *Financial Times* Ltd, October 15, 2016. Used under licence from the Financial Times.

Brexit mean for the territorial integrity of the UK, especially vis-à-vis an independence-minded but pro-EU Scotland, and the soft border in Ireland? How far can the UK prosper outside the EU single market? How will vital foreign investors such as Japan react? Are we a middle-ranking power on the edge of Europe doomed to relative decline or does Brexit offer Britain new opportunities as an agile trading nation, a sort of Venice of the 21st century or a giant Singapore?

Brexit is the biggest demerger in postwar history. Plenty of countries have joined the EU—28, to be precise—but none has actually left. No one knows the date when the UK will withdraw from the EU or the terms of divorce. We are sailing into uncharted territory.

And we are embarking on that journey at a moment of great peril. The international order of the past 70 years is fraying, maybe even breaking down. The Middle East offers the most obvious example of a shattered system. Further east, in the Pacific, the strategic question is whether China will seek, and achieve, a dominant position in the western Pacific, and how others, especially Japan, would react to such moves. Finally, the world watches with trepidation the US presidential election, a contest between the familiar (too familiar?) establishment candidate Hillary Clinton and the Muslim-baiting tycoon Donald Trump, who disdains traditional alliances and has a soft spot for strongmen like Vladimir Putin.

Between 1992 and 1998, I served as the FT's bureau chief in Brussels. I visited many European capitals, made life-long friends and reacquainted myself with European history and culture after six years in America. From my perch there, I had a bird's-eye view of the halting but successful march to economic and monetary union.

For the British, the European Community, as it was then known, was a bigger and better version of the European Free Trade Area, which we had co-founded in 1960. Unlike the French and Germans, scarred by three wars inside a century, we always saw Europe as an economic transaction rather than a political project.

In fact, the Maastricht treaty of 1992 fell well short of a federal Europe. It produced a hybrid political entity, which balanced greater supranational powers against looser intergovernmental co-operation. (The signatories promised "an ever-closer union"; but while the European spirit might have been willing, the flesh was not.)

Thus, Prime Minister John Major's government cannily secured several treaty opt-outs: from monetary union, justice and home affairs and the social chapter on the labour market. Britain along with France halted the federalists' ambitions in foreign and security policy. Germany was torn over surrendering the Deutschmark and resisted a full-blown political union, insisting on a Bundesbank design for the single currency with full central bank independence and no common fiscal policy.

Boris Johnson, then the charming and permanently dishevelled Brussels correspondent for the Daily Telegraph, pronounced Maastricht "game, set and match to John Major." But the press and a growing number of Eurosceptics continued to campaign against an all-powerful, centralised Europe. The later decision to invite 10 new members from central and eastern Europe further enhanced the concept of a multi-speed, multi-tiered union rather than a unitary or near-unitary federal set-up. Successive British governments did little to counter this chimera, still less to defend the importance of Britain's role in the EU, which on financial discipline, free trade and foreign policy was far more influential than imagined.

Fast forward to David Cameron's fateful decision in January 2013 to include a pledge to call a referendum on Brexit in the Conservative party manifesto ahead of the 2015 election. Many viewed this as an exercise in party management: the UK Independence party was gaining ground in the polls. Two Tory MPs (one appropriately named Reckless) had defected to Ukip. Mr Cameron was anxious to protect his right flank.

In fact, the referendum pledge owed much to a strategic repositioning of Britain within the EU, one little discussed or debated at the time. Essentially, Mr Cameron and George Osborne, then chancellor, took the view that the eurozone crisis which followed the financial crisis of 2008 would force members to integrate more closely. The UK, outside the single currency and with no intention of joining, would maintain a respectful distance: still an EU member but outside the core grouping.

As long as the UK could protect itself against discrimination, the government was relatively relaxed about a tighter continental club. True, Mr Osborne was heard to say, that while Britain would never again get a top job in Brussels, it would maintain influence in EU foreign and security matters. At the same time it would use its economic strength to go its own way in the world. Britain, it appeared, could have its cake and eat it in Europe.

History turned out very differently. In response to the financial crisis, there was no Great Leap Forward to political union in Europe. The eurozone group strengthened its own powers of crisis management but German-led resistance to further centralisation prevailed. There would be no common bond issuance or other measures to mutualise sovereign debt which were anathema to northern European creditor nations. After many stand-offs and much soul-searching, Greece was allowed to remain inside the monetary union, albeit on excruciating probationary terms.

This halfway house left the euro at risk, which is why the European Central Bank led by Mario Draghi stepped in with a pledge to do "whatever it takes" to support the single currency area via unconventional monetary policy. In effect, this was an insurance policy intended to buy time for Europe's political leaders while they took steps to revive their domestic economies.

Yet after seven years of crisis, the EU is left with a suboptimal currency area with staggeringly high unemployment, especially among the young, and terminally tepid growth. It is easy to blame Germany's insistence on imposing a fiscal straitjacket on its fellow euro members, but with the notable exceptions of Spain and Ireland, many countries have simply lacked the political will to reform their economies.

At the same time, almost all European countries have witnessed a rise in populist and anti-establishment parties at the expense of centrist and social democrat parties. We see radical leftism such as Podemos in Spain and Syriza in Greece, and hard-to-place insurgent movements such as Five Star in Italy, plus classic far-right parties that have rebranded themselves by downplaying anti-Semitism and playing up anti-immigration themes, such as Geert Wilders' Freedom Party in the Netherlands, the Front National in France led by Marine Le Pen, and Austria's Freedom Party.

To some degree, this can be explained in terms of the "squeezed middle," where globalisation and technological change have cut into the livelihoods of blue-collar workers and others in manufacturing.

More important is the migration crisis—the most serious the continent has faced since the late 1940s—which has gripped Europe these past three years. The flow of refugees, not just from the civil war in Syria but also from north Africa via the failed state of Libya, has almost overwhelmed the EU. And it has coincided with an outbreak of terrorist attacks by radical Islamists, notably in Belgium, France and latterly in Germany.

These twin crises have weakened, perhaps terminally, the authority of the most powerful leader in Europe: Angela Merkel. The German chancellor's uncharacteristically bold decision to welcome 1m refugees has triggered a political backlash at home and abroad. More broadly, migration has risen to a level where governments and the EU appear to have lost the ability to control their borders, a basic function of the nation state. Against this backdrop, Britons went to the polls on June 23.

The referendum on EU membership was an exercise in scaremongering by both sides. The Remain camp exaggerated the short-term economic costs of leaving and had nothing much else to say. The Leave campaign was mendacious—from the real net cost to the UK of EU membership to the false claim that Turkey would probably become a member by 2020.

Leave came up with a seductive slogan: take back control. It resonated with voters fearful about immigration, jobs and services.

Mr Cameron, who headed the Remain campaign, had no answer. Identity politics trumped economics.

Crucially, Mr Cameron insouciantly agreed to an up or down, all or nothing vote. He had pulled off a similar feat in 2014 in the referendum on Scottish independence. In retrospect, he should have borrowed from an earlier Scottish referendum in 1979 when the government insisted that 40 per cent of the electorate had to vote for a Scottish assembly before such devolution could go ahead.

So where does the June 23 vote leave Britain and its relationship with EU? Brexit means Brexit, declares Theresa May. But this does not take us very far. The Cameroons had no Plan B; even the Japanese government was better prepared for Brexit. Mrs May appears to have put controlling immigration and regaining national sovereignty at the top of her wishlist, ahead of defending the City of London and British business's access to the single market. She wants to trigger Article 50 to begin divorce proceedings by next March, putting Britain on course to exit the EU by 2019.

In the meantime, the government is trying to figure out the parameters for a new deal with Europe, a deal that will shape Britain's role in the world more profoundly than at any time since 1945.

I can think at least three plausible scenarios for Britain leaving the EU. None is appealing.

The first is an amicable divorce. All parties come to recognise the risks of things going badly wrong and make rational choices, bearing in mind economic interdependence and the weight of the UK economy. In the best of all possible worlds, the UK obtains some control over (but does not block) EU immigration—essentially putting in place safeguard mechanisms in light of the most serious migration and refugee crisis in decades. In return, Britain gets something approaching "equivalence" and can continue to access the single market as long as it complies with EU regulations.

Now I recognise that this is extraordinarily difficult to pull off given the interests of 27 other countries. The east Europeans will not take kindly to restrictions on the movement of labour, and continuing to comply with thousands of pages of EU regulations without input into new regulations may prove more difficult than at first glance. Moreover, many other west European countries may balk at Britain receiving terms that could be construed as an à la carte Europe.

Second, a quickie divorce: Brussels is not the new Las Vegas, but there is a view in London which argues that the UK should move early and decisively towards exit. Under this short, sharp scenario, now said to be favoured by Mr Johnson, the UK foreign secretary, and Liam Fox, the trade minister, Britain would reject post-exit deals with the EU. Mr Fox says he wants the UK to leave the EU customs union and negotiate bilateral trade deals with other nations, independent of EU terms and conditions.

Economists for Brexit admit this option would involve tariffs on UK manufacturing exports but it would have the advantage of clarity, albeit a somewhat brutal clarity. In the medium-term, the UK economy would end up specialising in services and lose manufacturing. Yet as my colleague Martin Wolf argued in the run-up to Brexit, to eliminate all bargaining chips seems wildly implausible. We are not Hong Kong or Singapore—small entities that lack competitive democratic politics. "It is far more likely," wrote Mr Wolf, "that a supposedly autonomous UK would be more protectionist and interventionist than it is in the EU."

The third scenario is a hostile or sloppy divorce. This is undesirable but eminently possible. Negotiations between the UK and EU soon become acrimonious. Every country has a pet cause to protect or advance, and the negotiations prove fiendishly complex —enlargement in reverse, as it were. A stand-off ensues: financial markets are spooked, bond yields start to spike, consumer sentiment crashes. The UK and European economies slip into recession.

At this point, Mrs May has a choice: does she tough it out and walk out of the EU with an imperfect deal or does she acknowledge that Brexit has delivered an outcome that is manifestly not in the interests of the UK and resubmit the matter to the British people, not necessarily in a referendum but in a general election?

We should also consider that the EU itself may look rather different than it does today. In the next two years, a host of national elections could usher in a new guard. I am not suggesting Ms Le Pen will win next spring and bring about Frexit, or that Ms Merkel will lose in the German election in a year's time. But the political dynamic in Europe is more fluid than first appears.

My colleague Gideon Rachman has raised another possibility: a two-tier Europe with a core around Germany, Belgium, Italy, Spain and, most likely but not absolutely certainly, France. Other countries, not just the Visegrad Four of central Europe but also the Nordics and possibly the Netherlands, would have a somewhat looser relationship with access to the single market and co-operation on foreign policy. Yet another scenario is that one or several EU countries may simply choose to leave along with the UK.

Yet none of this is certain. And if the EU does change, precedent suggests it will do so slowly. In my view, it would be infinitely preferable if all sides took decisions that would have direct benefits for their citizens. In the case of the EU, this means boosting job creation, regaining control of borders and winning back public confidence.

Back in 1877, Lord Salisbury, then UK prime minister, wrote a letter to Lord Lytton, then viceroy of India, in which he said: "English policy is to float lazily downstream, occasionally putting out a diplomatic boathook to avoid collisions."

This lazy mantra will not do for Britain in 2016. The next five years will undoubtedly be bumpy. There are no easy answers to our European dilemma. The EU may adapt in response to Brexit and its own manifest failings but that change will come slowly. We cannot afford to pursue the politics of inertia.

The big question is: Are we sliding toward being a middle-ranking power on the edge of Europe doomed to relative prosperity and gradual decline, or does Brexit offer Britain new opportunities as an agile trading nation, a sort of Venice of the 21st century or a giant Atlantic Singapore?

Since the end of the Cold War, many fine minds have tried to conceptualise the UK's place in the world. Tony Blair, former prime minister, described Britain as a "transatlantic bridge" which worked well until Iraq when the UK sided with the US against an antiwar coalition led by France, Germany and Russia. David Miliband, former foreign secretary, cast Britain as a "global hub," a magnet for commerce, culture, education and finance. Most recently, Mr Cameron talked about the UK as an island nation adapting to a new "networked world."

Yet even assuming that Britain leaves the EU, it surely cannot stand aside from Europe. The UK remains a member of Nato and the G8; along with France, it has the most serious military fighting force in western Europe.

Brexit offers an opportunity to redefine our role in a new world where the economic centre of gravity is shifting away from the old European continent eastward to Asia. Britain must look to its comparative advantages in a new world. It has a world-class economy, which, with its flexible labour market, has performed better than most in Europe in terms of growth and job creation —more than 2m since 2010.

Britain is a world-class financial centre. The City has also thrived because London, despite its sky-high house prices, is a cool place to live, work and, yes, eat in restaurants. That's why tens of thousands of EU citizens—French, Italian, German, Spanish —live there.

Britain is developing world-class technologies. The country boasts a vibrant research community where science and technology thrive. It has world-class universities, cultural institutions and creative industries; a world-class workforce drawn to the opportunities of an innovative, multicultural society.

The UK also has world-class defence and intelligence capabilities. Of course, on internal security matters such as tackling crime and terrorism, it benefits from co-operation and intelligence-sharing with its European counterparts.

The Left Wing Case for Brexit (One Day)

The leftwing case for Brexit is strategic and clear. The EU is not—and cannot become—a democracy. Instead, it provides the most hospitable ecosystem in the developed world for rentier monopoly corporations, tax-dodging elites and organised crime. It has an executive so powerful it could crush the leftwing government of Greece; a legislature so weak that it cannot effectively determine laws or control its own civil service. A judiciary that, in the Laval and Viking judgments, subordinated workers' right to strike to an employer's right do business freely.

Its central bank is committed, by treaty, to favour deflation and stagnation over growth. State aid to stricken industries is prohibited. The austerity we deride in Britain as a political choice is, in fact, written into the EU treaty as a non-negotiable obligation. So are the economic principles of the Thatcher era. A Corbyn-led Labour government would have to implement its manifesto in defiance of EU law.

[...]

All this suggests that those of us who want Brexit in order to reimpose democracy, promote social justice and subordinate companies to the rule of law should bide our time. But here's the price we will pay. Hungary is one electoral accident away from going fascist; the French conservative elite is one false move away from handing the presidency to the Front National; in Austria the far-right FPÖ swept the first round of the presidential polls. Geert Wilders's virulently Islamophobic PVV is leading the Dutch opinion polls.

The EU's economic failure is fuelling racism and the ultra right.

— "The leftwing case for Brexit (one day)," by Paul Mason, The *Guardian*, May 16, 2016.

These strengths derive from native brainpower but they also benefit from the free flow of talented individuals from overseas. Our universities have benefited financially from overseas students, even more so from academics coming to work from abroad, from China, India, the US and Europe.

Our choice is stark: do we shrink into Little England turning inward and becoming poorer in every sense of the word, or do we look outward, drawing on our innate resourcefulness and engaging positively in the world as a medium-sized power with a sound economy, an Atlantic Singapore?

I vote for the second option. A strong, open UK—with a close relationship with Europe and the US—acting as a powerful magnet for business and commerce and a voice for a reinvigorated liberal order against the forces of anti-globalisation and nationalism. This will require patience, political will and leadership—but can we do it? Yes, we can.

Viewpoint 3

In the UK, Euroscepticism Is Nothing New

Daniel P. Vajdich

The UK has a superiority complex, according to senior fellow at the Future Europe Initiative Daniel Vajdich in the following viewpoint. After World War II, the UK prized its "special relationship" with the United States over any European alliance. That is in part why, in the middle of the twentieth century, French president Charles de Gaulle stonewalled Britain's bid to join the European Economic Community (EEC). The Brits, he said, were inward and "peculiar." When the UK did eventually make it in to the EEC, it tried to tower over its neighbors. Whatever present-day issues sparked Brexit—immigration, populism, misfortune—the UK's historic unease with Europe provided the kindling.

There has been a near total absence of historical context since the United Kingdom voted to leave the European Union in June. The British have had a tortured relationship with European integration for several decades now. In 1945, after two global conflicts had concluded on the European continent in twenty-five years, some European (and many American) policymakers began the process of bringing Europe together in way that would spawn unprecedented interdependence and thus reduce the likelihood of yet another major war. Winston Churchill famously espoused a "United States of Europe," but he did not intend for the UK to be a part of it.

"The UK has never wished to be part of the European project," by Daniel P. Vajdich, The National Interest, August 15, 2016. Reprinted by Permission.

The British were never enthusiastic about this process. Even collective defense and the creation of NATO—both hailed today by most proponents of Brexit—were viewed with skepticism by UK political elites and many citizens in the wake of World War Two, despite their clear-eyed appreciation of the emerging Soviet threat. While British leaders saw the value and necessity of European unification, the United Kingdom was skeptical of its own participation in continental integration projects.

Two factors drove these sentiments. First, the UK wanted to safeguard what Churchill called its "special relationship" with the United States. Less than a year later, London notified the United States of its inability to finance Greece and Turkey in the face of internal communist threats and external Soviet pressure. It was now clear that the UK's younger cousin would inherit leadership of the Western world and spearhead its confrontation with Soviet communism. A collective Europe with the UK as its member would surely undermine the special relationship it was thought.

Second, the British Empire would soon be greatly reduced, but its leaders refused to engage in a corresponding adjustment of their imperial mentality. After being the world's most dominant nation for over three centuries, the British did not want to be treated as just another European country—neither victorious but war-torn France, nor vanquished Germany. They would not allow themselves to be dragged into a nebulous union to advance the interests of others, that is, in order to assuage French fears of long-term German domination and help create conditions that would justify U.S. withdrawal from Europe.

The latter was certainly on the minds of American policymakers at the time. It was neither their desire nor their intention immediately after WWII to maintain a large U.S. troop presence in Europe and to keep European countries dependent on the United States. They soon concluded that the rapid political, economic and military revitalization of Europe could only be achieved on the basis of European integration, which was far more likely to succeed with British involvement. The United States put substantial pressure on the UK to take part in Europe's unification. It succeeded with respect to collective security and NATO—only because the United States itself was willing to join, which preserved the special relationship—but failed to convince London to participate in the European Coal and Steel Community (ECSC) and the European Economic Community (EEC).

Both Labour and Conservative governments under Clement Attlee and Anthony Eden declined to participate in the creation of a common European market. But by the late 1950s the UK's attitude toward Europe and its economic integration project had shifted. This shift, however, was on pragmatic rather than philosophical grounds. The British did not suddenly see the merits of European integration like the French and Germans who viewed continental union as a way to achieve stability and—for the Gaullists at least—independence from the United States. The British viewed the European project almost purely in the context of economic growth. While European output surged in the decade after hostilities ended the British economy sputtered and could not seem to gain traction.

In 1961, the European common market looked far more attractive to the UK than it did just several years prior. That year the Conservative government of Harold Macmillan formally applied to the join the EEC. While Macmillan seemed to embrace the economic and even political rationale behind European integration, he also emphasized the importance of UK relations with the rest of the world and told the House of Commons:

> *"I believe that it is both our duty and our interest to contribute towards that strength by securing the closest possible unity within Europe. At the same time, if a closer relationship between the United Kingdom and the countries of the European Economic Community were to disrupt the long-standing and historic ties between the United Kingdom and the other nations of the Commonwealth the loss would be greater than the gain. The Commonwealth is a great source of stability and strength both to Western Europe and to the world as a whole, and I am sure*

> *that its value is fully appreciated by the member Governments of the European Economic Community."*

Because of his concerns related to the UK's special relationship with the United States and its global rather than European focus, Charles de Gaulle vetoed British EEC membership in 1961 and again in 1967 when it applied to join under Harold Wilson's Labour government. De Gaulle explained his decision:

> *"Britain is insular, maritime, bound up by its trade, its markets, its food supplies, with the most varied and often the most distant countries. Her activity is essentially industrial and commercial, not agricultural. She has, in all her work, very special, and original habits and traditions. In short, the nature, structure, circumstances peculiar to England are very different from those of other continentals. How can Britain, in the way that she lives, produces, trades, be incorporated into the Common Market as it has been conceived and functions?"*

Conservative Prime Minister Edward Heath established a close relationship with de Gaulle's successor Georges Pompidou who eventually lifted French objections and in 1973 the UK finally joined what would later become the EU. Already in 1975, however, Wilson returned to Downing Street and retained his pledge to hold a referendum on EEC membership, despite having advocated for accession and filing an application during his previous mandate. Labour argued that the Conservatives had negotiated poor terms for UK membership and worried that EEC rules would prevent the party from pursuing leftist industrial policies.

Foreign Secretary John Callaghan also opposed the notion of European Union, which he described as "quite unrealistic and not desired by our peoples, certainly not by the British people." He said that the UK was "deeply concerned about the politics of the [European Economic] Community; about the broad direction which it is going to take both in its international development and in its relations with other countries and group of countries." Callaghan emphasized that the UK wanted to "remain a member of an effective Atlantic Alliance" and expressed concern about disagreements between the EEC and the United States.

In its 1974 election platform Labour promised to renegotiate the terms of EEC membership and then arrange a referendum to determine whether the UK would continue to participate in the Common Market. Although French Foreign Minister Jean Sauvagnargues called the UK's objectives "wholly contrary to the very spirit of the community," by March 1975, London had successfully convinced the eight other member states and European Commission to revise the Common Agricultural Policy (CAP), grant the UK a refund of 125 million pounds because of "unfair" budgetary practices, and provide several other assurances regarding Labour's continued ability to pursue "full employment." Parliament overwhelmingly approved the renegotiation 396–170 and over 67 percent of Britons voted to remain in the EEC.

Much like the recent Brexit vote, the 1975 referendum was supported by a vast majority of parliamentarians, but it sharply divided the party and cabinet that organized the ballot. Soon thereafter, however, Labour decisively gravitated away from Euroskepticism and began to strongly favor European integration. The leftist elements of Labour who were previously worried about Europe's encroachment on their authority to subsidize particular industries, and sectors of the economy realized that the Commission could serve as an ally rather than foe when it came to protecting the interests of the party's electorate. As Labour became increasingly supportive of the European project and the UK's role in it, the Conservatives, who had led the UK into Europe and almost unanimously supported continued EEC membership during the referendum, started to move in an anti-European direction.

Enter Margaret Thatcher. She took the helm of the Conservative Party in 1975 and four years later became prime minister. Among her qualms with the EEC, Thatcher believed that London still contributed disproportionately more to the Community budget than it received in benefits. At the time the UK was the second poorest member state and did not have a large agriculture sector, which was particularly salient because most of the budget was spent on CAP. On the basis of this Thatcher successfully negotiated an annual rebate in 1984 that has lowered the UK's contribution to common budget since then.

In her 1988 Bruges speech Thatcher affirmed, "Britain does not dream of some cozy, isolated existence on the fringes of the European Community. Our destiny is in Europe, as part of the Community." But she also argued for a limited form of European integration that recognized the preeminence of sovereignty. Thatcher declared:

> *"My first guiding principle is this: willing and active cooperation between independent sovereign states is the best way to build a successful European Community. To try to suppress nationhood and concentrate power at the center of a European conglomerate would be highly damaging and would jeopardize the objectives we seek to achieve . . . We have not successfully rolled back the frontiers of the state in Britain, only to see them reimposed at a European level with a European super-state exercising a new dominance from Brussels."*

Over a decade prior to Thatcher's speech and a few years after the collapse of the Bretton Woods system, EEC countries established the European Monetary System (EMS) in an initiative to bind their currencies and stabilize exchange rates. A weighted basket of European currencies called the European Exchange Rate Mechanism (ERM) was used to determine exchange rates and restrict fluctuations within fixed margins.

The UK, however, opted out of ERM and did not join until 1990—albeit only briefly. That year exchange controls were abolished and capital movements fully liberalized. But the pound quickly came under strong pressure from foreign exchange investors like George Soros and the UK withdrew from ERM two years later. The Bank of England spent over 6 billion pounds to keep the currency within the mandated exchange rate margins during this period.

In 1992, the EEC became the EU when the Maastricht Treaty was adopted. This treaty for the first time established Common Foreign and Security Policy (CFSP) and Justice and Home Affairs (JHA) integration pillars. It also generated the Maastricht convergence criteria for member states to enter the third and final stage of Economic and Monetary Union (EMU)—that is, adoption of the common euro currency. Still in deep recession and having recently been forced out of ERM, the UK opted out of EMU and JHA. Five years later London also definitively opted to remain outside the Schengen zone area when the common travel area was made part of the Amsterdam Treaty.

Since then, the UK's positions on many issues—from the CFSP to regulatory questions—have often diverged from most if not all other EU member states. Its relations with the EU and attitudes toward European integration have at no time been characterized by unqualified enthusiasm. The uniqueness of these attitudes is derived from the UK's unique history and its own form of British exceptionalism.

Unlike the French and Germans who genuinely believed in the merits of the European project the majority of Brits never did. The decision to apply to the EEC and join in 1973 was a wholly pragmatic decision devoid of ideology. And the decision to leave the EU is no different. It is true that existing challenges in the EU—migration, terrorism and democratic deficits—all shaped this pragmatism and its conclusions, ultimately leading a majority of the British people to favor Brexit. But so too did the events of the 1960s and 1970s that led Brits to support membership at a time when EEC economies were growing rapidly while the UK was seen as the sick man of Europe.

These roles are in essence reversed today. And having no strong ideological belief in European integration the UK made a pragmatic choice to separate itself from a community to which is has never truly belonged. Brexit should not doom the European project, which together with NATO has kept peace for over seventy years on one of the most violent continents in human history.

In the wake of Brexit, the UK will soon join the United States as a country that is not a participant in the project but nonetheless has a core interest in its success. Both must now work with the EU to ensure this success.

Viewpoint 4

Was Brexit Really About Race?

Leah Donnella

Bigotry, racism, and nativism animated the Leavers' cause. So writes National Public Radio reporter Lena Donnella in the following viewpoint. Critics have shown that the UK Independence Party (UKIP), which advocated Britain's defection from the EU, spent years fomenting racial anxiety. The fear of immigrants—regardless of the fact that, by and large, they enliven the culture and enhance the economy—may not have caused Brexit all on its own, but it was a key factor. For that reason, Donnella writes, UKIP's venomous propaganda merits scrutiny.

On Thursday night, the votes poured in: After months of debate, the United Kingdom officially voted to leave the European Union in a referendum nicknamed "Brexit."

Shortly after the results were made public, Prime Minister David Cameron announced that he would leave office in October. Global stocks tanked, and the British pound crashed to a 31-year low. World leaders from the U.S. to Japan to Germany spoke out about the far-reaching effects the referendum would have.

The scale of this reaction was predictable—after all, the U.K. joined the EU's predecessor, the EEC (European Economic Community), back in 1973 and has been one of its most influential members for decades. As the (now formerly!) fifth-largest economy in the world, even moderate changes in Britain's political stance affect global markets.

So why did the U.K. vote for something so politically and economically disruptive? Some say race has a lot to do with it —specifically, the racial tension that has resulted from the U.K.'s recently welcoming in record numbers of immigrants. In 2015, 630,000 foreign national migrants came to the U.K. from both inside and outside the EU. This year, the U.K. has ushered in an additional 333,000.

The campaign to get the U.K. to leave the EU (also known as the "Leave" campaign) was spearheaded by the right-wing, populist UK Independence Party, or UKIP. The party, led by Member in the European Parliament Nigel Farage, says that the EU "means the end of the UK as an independent, self-governing nation with its own government and its own borders.'"

For months, UKIP has fought for the United Kingdom's independence from the EU—some say by capitalizing on racially charged animus toward immigrants. In the *Washington Post,* writer Anyusha Rose points to the Leave campaign as evidence that in the U.K., "racism is no longer racism—it's legitimate opinion."

Areeq Chowdhury, a British writer and the founder of WebRoots Democracy, said last week that it's "important we remember that this is a referendum that has only been made possible due to a long, hard-fought campaign by those on the far-right and political movements ridden with allegations of bigotry, xenophobia, and racism." He continues:

> *"Nigel Farage—the UKIP leader who once said that his party 'would never win the nigger vote,' refers to Chinese takeaways as 'a chinky,' and said people would feel 'concerned' to live next to Romanians—is the man who should take a significant chunk of the credit for us having this referendum. It was his party's success in the European Parliament elections, as well as defections which he brokered from the Conservative Party, which has led us to this point today."*

Zack Beauchamp over at Vox writes that the UKIP has spent the past 10 years "focusing, obsessively, on the threat from immigrants, from both inside the EU and out."

That work seems to have been fruitful. Beauchamp says, "Over the course of the past 20 years, the percentage of Britons ranking 'immigration/race relations' as among the country's most important issues has gone from near zero percent to about 45 percent. Seventy-seven percent of Brits today believe that immigration levels should be reduced."

Many politicians say anti-immigration sentiment shouldn't necessarily be cast as racism—they argue that immigrants take jobs from native-born British citizens, that immigration drives down wages for everyone, and that the desire to keep jobs abundant and wages high is a goal that millions share, across racial and political lines.

And Timothy B. Lee, at Vox, argues that there are compelling reasons that British voters might have decided to leave the EU besides immigration—including the weakness of the euro and the EU's entrenched corporate interests. Still, concern about the rate of immigration is central to Lee's list.

But James Bloodworth, writing for *International Business Times,* says the issue can't be explained in purely economic terms. Even as the number of migrants arriving in the U.K. rose to a record 333,000 in May of this year, immigrants have been an overall boon to the British economy. Bloodworth explains:

> *"Hostility to immigration—and by extension hostility to Europe —is driven by cultural concerns as much as by economic worries. That's certainly what the University of Oxford's Migration Observatory has been saying in recent years. It has pointed out on a number of occasions that cultural concerns better explain negative attitudes towards migration than a person's economic position. In essence it is about whether England feels like England."*

J.K. Rowling, author of the *Harry Potter* series, cautions against casting everyone who backed the Leave movement as a bigot but also writes about the danger of painting immigrants as monsters and villains:

> *"Leave has been busy threatening us with another monster: a tsunami of faceless foreigners heading for our shores, among them rapists and terrorists.*
>
> *"It is dishonourable to suggest, as many have, that Leavers are all racists and bigots: they aren't and it is shameful to suggest that they are. Nevertheless, it is equally nonsensical to pretend that racists and bigots aren't flocking to the 'Leave' cause, or that they aren't, in some instances, directing it. For some of us, that fact alone is enough to give us pause. The picture of Nigel Farage standing in front of a poster showing a winding line of Syrian refugees captioned 'Breaking Point' is, as countless people have already pointed out, an almost exact duplicate of propaganda used by the Nazis."*

Some British politicians are trying to soften the blow. Sadiq Khan, the mayor of London, wrote a message on his Facebook page telling EU residents living in London that they are welcome and that the city is grateful for them.

Lauren Hansen, a writer at *The Week,* wrote, "Mayor Khan's comments are especially poignant in this post-Brexit world as the continent's largest city grapples with the tension between an anti-immigration sentiment and the diversity that makes London, and cities like it, thrive both economically and culturally."

Of course, it would be remiss not to mention the parallels that many are drawing between the Brexit movement and Donald Trump's campaign rhetoric. Trump has publicly supported Britain's vote to leave the EU, and folks told NPR's Frank Langfitt that "similar issues—globalization and economics—are driving the Brexit and U.S. presidential campaigns."

In an article called "What Do The Brexit Movement And Donald Trump Have In Common?" the *New Yorker*'s John Cassidy wrote:

> *"Certainly, a parallel factor in both men's rise is racism, or, more specifically, nativism. Trump has presented a nightmarish vision of America overrun by Mexican felons and Muslim terrorists.*

UKIP printed up campaign posters that showed thousands of dark-colored refugees lining up to enter Slovenia, which is part of the E.U., next to the words 'breaking point: The EU has failed us all.' "

In the months to come, the U.S. will have the advantage of seeing how this vote plays out in the U.K. before voting in its own presidential elections in November.

Viewpoint 5

Brexit and the Legacy of British Colonialism

Laleh Khalili

In the following viewpoint, Middle Eastern politics professor Laleh Khalili argues we must consider Brexit in relation to the intractable xenophobia of England's centuries-long colonial endeavor. First, Khalili critiques the cliché analyses of the Leavers' success. Next, Khalili—who teaches at the School of Oriental and African Studies at the University of London—shows how advocates of the Leave campaign had to correct their campaign hyperbole post-hoc. Finally, and most importantly, she argues that "the long and brutal history of British colonialism and empire lies at the heart of so much British insularity and racism."

Theoretically, there was a progressive case to be made for Britain exiting the European Union via the referendum held on June 23, 2016. But the campaign for Brexit—the infelicitous name given the political process—was, from the very first, fought on the grounds of xenophobia and racism. Moreover, what has transpired in Britain since the Leave campaign won has only shown how easily the veneer of civility and conviviality can be peeled back to reveal the virulence of racism and xenophobia seething under the skin of British social life.

Britain was never a part of the eurozone. Therefore, the extensive austerity measures that its Tory/Liberal Democrat coalition government of 2010-2015 put into place, and that the

---

"After Brexit: Reckoning With Britain's Racism and Xenophobia," by Laleh Khalili, Truthout, June 30, 2016. http://www.truth-out.org/opinion/item/36651-after-brexit-reckoning-with-britain-s-racism-and-xenophobia.

Tory government of 2015 ratcheted up, were its own doing. That said, the austerity measures emanating from the more financially powerful EU states—Germany and France—and imposed upon and massively affecting the economies of countries such as Greece and Portugal were on the forefront of every British progressive's mind before the EU referendum. It is possible to be a member of the EU and not part of the eurozone monetary sphere—as is the case with the UK, alongside Bulgaria, Croatia, Czech Republic, Denmark, Hungary, Poland, Romania and Sweden.

The EU itself is a massive bureaucratic mechanism, institutional machine and ideological apparatus devised to facilitate the movement of capital, goods, services and people across its internal borders. The free—or relatively unrestricted—movement of goods and capital without encountering tariffs or protection barriers has resulted in the further consolidation of the power of the big manufacturers in Europe as well as unfettered growth in and institutional protection of the financial and banking sector. The EU legal bodies legislate around or regulate some of this free trade, but generally decide in favor of big business over trade unions.

The EU's "empire of free trade" has been the target of the ire of both the right and the left; the right is incensed over the regulations seen to hamper businesses (especially environmental and health-and-safety regulations as well as the human rights charter) and the left is incensed over the unaccountability of the EU officials and its rigid neoliberal stance. This undemocratic power exercised by distant Eurocrats is the plausible basis of a progressive criticism of the institution.

But what has distinguished the EU free-trade pact from other free-trade pacts—notably the North American Free Trade Agreement—is the relatively unrestricted movement of people across internal European borders to seek jobs or residency elsewhere in the Union. And it is this free movement of people that has triggered a long festering xenophobia at the heart of British society.

Britain's insularity has been punctured throughout its history in moments where the need for migrant labor has trumped the Little Englander aversion toward foreigners. One such moment was the post-Second World War reconstruction era when the devastated country needed people to aid in the reconstruction of the national economy (much like the rest of Europe). The importation of guest workers from the colonies, followed by decolonization and the migration of former colonized subjects to the metropole have triggered virulent xenophobic and racist responses in Britain. That the British political classes have refused to reckon with the country's colonial legacy and their steadfast refusal to acknowledge the racism interwoven in its institutions have only exacerbated this xenophobia and racism.

This xenophobia takes different shapes according to the historical moment, but neoliberal policies have only ever intensified these sentiments. Migrants are today blamed for taking up places in housing and schools, burdening the country's publicly-funded universal health system and weakening the working class. Scant attention is paid to how, beginning with Margaret Thatcher's scorched-earth neoliberalism, policies of privatization and austerity —during both feast and famine—have led to a degradation of national life, a diminishing of social mobility and a growth in inequality in the UK.

In the 1990s, under the reign of Tony Blair's New Labour, Thatcher's policies continued in new guises: the fiercely beloved National Health Service (NHS) was funded, but often via public-private partnerships that have in fact burdened the NHS with serious debt and crumbling infrastructures, while enriching private investors and developers. Instead of preserving unused schools, local councils were encouraged to sell off their school buildings in the 1990s, again benefiting property developers who turned these attractive Victorian structures into high-end housing without anticipating the acute future need for school buildings and school places. The sale of social housing, which had been a pillar of Thatcherite policy of privatization, has been exacerbated by wholly inadequate construction of new affordable housing and no effort to replace the stock of social housing lost under Thatcher.

The privatization of the efficient national rail, electricity, phone and water infrastructures has been a boon to profiteering private firms, while the basic transport and utility infrastructures have deteriorated, and their costs—especially of commuting—have become exorbitant. The replacement of manufacturing jobs with service jobs, the destruction of the mining and shipping sectors, and the weakening of trade union protections—particularly in the more militant sectors—have also had massively detrimental effects on vast swathes of Britain's industrial areas.

It is no matter that the Tory Party (under its official name the Conservatives) is ostensibly a party of both fiscal and social conservatism, that the Liberal Democrats are ostensibly a party of social liberalism and fiscal conservatism, and that Labour is a self-avowed socialist party (though subjected to neoliberal reforms under Tony Blair, New Labour moved to the center as did many other social democratic parties in Europe). In the face of rising popular discontent with this abasement of social life in the UK, it has been easier for politicians across the political spectrum to displace the blame for these policies to vulnerable migrants rather than to acknowledge the role not only of the Conservative (Tory) Party (and for a while, its Liberal Democratic coalition partners), but also of the Labour Party in bringing about this turn of events. In this regards, Labour has been wholly complicit in pandering to xenophobic sentiments in order to deflect blame from New Labour policies.

These policies of austerity and attendant anti-migrant sentiments have occurred in the context of ever more intense hysteria around the question of "terror." We live in a time of legislations on radicalization, particularly the absurdly authoritarian "Prevent" laws, practices of surveillance not only of Muslims, but also of "suspicious" talk in schools, universities, hospitals and public places, and counterterrorism operations. These government measures—and particularly the Prevent legislation, which makes it mandatory for school and university teachers to spy on their students and any public official to look out for signs of "radicalization" among Muslim youths in particular—have led to criminalization of entire communities, and an increase in the sense of vulnerability among British citizens and residents of Muslim origin.

This convergence of anti-migrant xenophobia and Islamophobic racism has now become the most recognizable feature of politics in Britain and have shaped successive election campaigns. Parliamentary elections, especially since 2010, have often pivoted around the question of migration. Although in the 2015 elections, Nigel Farage's right-wing anti-immigration and Eurosceptic party, UK Independence Party (UKIP), only secured one seat in the parliament, he nevertheless picked up millions of votes and Farage managed to define the discourse around migration. So much so, that in pandering to UKIP's base, David Cameron announced the EU referendum.

The London mayoral election, held a scant eight weeks before the EU referendum, was another example of this ignominious turn. The campaign between Labour's Sadiq Khan, a liberal Muslim leaning toward New Labour, and the Tories' Zac Goldsmith, until then best known for his environmental campaigning, showed the extent to which even the more ostensibly liberal members of the Tory Party would appeal to this seam of racism and Islamophobia in order to win votes. This all came to a head with the referendum, where all other issues faded into the background and migration and anti-Muslim sentiments (the latter of which does not have a logical relation to the EU in any case) became the central axis around which the referendum pivoted.

Although the outcome was not really foreseen, and although the end result of the referendum was fairly close (52 percent for Leave; 48 percent for Remain), the win for Eurosceptics took even Leave voters by surprise.

The most prevalent cliché of post-referendum analysis has been that the vote for exit should be read as a "working-class revolt."

Setting aside the unspoken assumption that this rebellious working class must by definition be white, the post-referendum exit polls actually indicate the "working-class" characterization of the Leave vote is inaccurate. It is true that a higher percentage of working-class voters voted for exit than did upper- and middle-class voters —46 percent versus 64 percent. But once turnout by class was taken into account, the numbers looked different. As Ben Pritchett's calculations (along with his caveats about the turnout numbers including anomalies) have shown, the far greater turnout of the middle and upper classes, versus the working class—90 percent versus 52 percent—meant that in absolute numbers, a far higher number of middle- and upper-class voters (around 10 million voters) actually voted to Leave the EU than the working class (approximately 7 million voters), many others of whom abstained from voting.

Lord Ashcroft's exit polls showed that if voters thought that multiculturalism, feminism, social liberalism, the environmental movement and immigration are forces for ill, they voted overwhelmingly to leave the EU. The same polls showed that while 53 percent of voters who described themselves as white and 58 percent of those who described themselves as Christian voted to leave the EU, more than two-thirds of Asian voters, nearly three-quarters of Black voters and 70 percent of self-identified Muslims voted to remain in the EU.

Only hours after their win, the Eurosceptic leaders had already backpedaled on some of their most major promises. Nigel Farage claimed that he never agreed with the claim—emblazoned on the side of a campaign bus used by Eurosceptic leaders—that the £350 billion weekly payments formerly paid to the EU would actually be used to fund the NHS. Iain Duncan-Smith's weaker claim was that only after the EU agricultural subsidies (to the Tory heartlands) were replaced would any leftover funds be divided between the NHS and other needs. The irony was of course that many of those agricultural heartlands had been in receipt of more handouts from the EU than other places in the UK.

Claims that the UK fisheries could benefit from a post-EU deregulation were similarly walked back. Even on migration, which had played such a decisive and divisive role in the referendum, the Eurosceptic leaders were already tempering their claims. These retreats from promises have been so blatant that the Leave campaign has simply wiped the archive of all their opinion pieces and documents from the web.

Even more astonishing is how the Leave camp seems not to have planned at all for an eventual exit. There is no certainty as to when—or even whether—Article 50 (a provision of Treaty of Lisbon which provides for EU member countries leaving) will ever be invoked, setting into motion two years of negotiations that will allow Britain to unravel its legislations, trade arrangements, migration processes and regulations from the EU.

Perhaps the most worrying fallout of the referendum vote, however, has been the extraordinary spike in violence against migrants and non-white British citizens and residents. Although many—if not most—of those who voted for Leave did not do so out of xenophobic or racist reasons, the vote seems to have legitimated an extraordinary outburst of such attacks against migrants—especially those from Poland—and non-white British citizens, residents, and visitors.

There is very little that promises an abatement of such racism. The immediate economic fallout of the Leave vote will only exacerbate the sense of economic uncertainty, possibly leading to a recession. The weakening of the pound will inevitably lead to a rise in price of imports (which will be exacerbated by the implementation of tariffs once the UK leaves the EU). Massive losses in the stock market have wiped vast amounts off pensions, giving yet more alibis to the state and private pension providers for reducing what is available to retirees. Rating agencies' downgrading of UK's ability to borrow will lead to higher borrowing costs for the UK government and a growth in UK deficit, which of course provides an excuse for further austerity measures and an increase in taxes (which Tory governments of course will not levy against

Fences: A Brexit Diary

What does this vote mean? What was it really about? Immigration? Inequality? Historic xenophobia? Sovereignty? EU bureaucracy? Anti-neoliberal revolution? Class war?

[...]

A referendum magnifies the worst aspects of an already imperfect system—democracy—channeling a dazzlingly wide variety of issues through a very narrow gate. It has the appearance of intensification—Ultimate democracy! Thumbs up or thumbs down!—but in practice delivers a dangerously misleading reduction. Even many who voted Leave ended up feeling that their vote did not accurately express their feelings. They had a wide variety of motives for their vote, and much of the Remain camp was similarly splintered.

[...]

[T]he notable feature of neoliberalism is that it feels like you can do nothing to change it, but this vote offered up the rare prize of causing a chaotic rupture in a system that more usually steamrolls all in its path. But even this most optimistic leftist interpretation—that this was a violent, more or less considered reaction to austerity and the neoliberal economic meltdown that preceded it—cannot deny the casual racism that seems to have been unleashed alongside it, both by the campaign and by the vote itself.

[...]

One useful consequence of Brexit is to finally and openly reveal a deep fracture in British society that has been thirty years in the making. The gaps between north and south, between the social classes, between Londoners and everyone else, between rich Londoners and poor Londoners, and between white and brown and black are real and need to be confronted by all of us, not only those who voted Leave.

—"Fences: A Brexit Diary," by Zadie Smith, NYREV, Inc., August 18, 2016.

the corporations or the richest earners). The revocation of EU protections for migrant workers means that while the UK will continue to see migration from the EU countries, these workers will not be protected from the worst depredations of unscrupulous employers. As labor studies scholar Roland Erne has argued, this degradation of migrant worker rights will only accelerate the race to the bottom for *all workers*, both migrant and British. Nor will parliamentary politics in England provide any respite.

Already, politicians from Scotland and Northern Ireland (both of which voted overwhelmingly to Remain in the EU) are talking of a second independence referendum and a reunification of Ireland, respectively, in order to remain in the EU. The rump state that would remain if such fragmentation occurred would likely have a much strengthened Tory government and a Labour Party that would have difficulty winning.

In a coming recession, with intensified inequality, rising poverty and stalled social mobility, under a Tory government which has no stakes in egalitarian social policies, racism and xenophobia, right-wing populism, ultranationalist ideologies, even fascism will find a fertile soil. The horrifying racist and xenophobic attacks of the last week are haunted by the "rivers of blood" racism of yesteryears. In a now notorious 1968 speech, the Tory MP Enoch Powell promised rivers of blood to a country in which migration had led to "the Black man [having] the whip hand over the white man." UKIP's Nigel Farage has never hidden his admiration for Enoch Powell, and even the anti-immigrant views of many in the Tory Party are shaped by Powell.

The long and brutal history of British colonialism and empire lies at the heart of so much British insularity and racism. The deep roots of this racism will likely influence the politics of tomorrow, as it has already done that of today. To counter such a bleak future, mass mobilization is necessary—and any form of progressive mass mobilization has to recognize that class politics are always articulated through a politics of race. Reckoning with Britain's racism and xenophobia across time, place, parties and social classes is the necessary first step in such mobilization.

Viewpoint 6

Brexit Didn't Happen Overnight

Tsvi Bisk

For the student of history, the past sorts itself into a sensible sequence of events. At least it does for author and Israeli futurist Tsvi Bisk in the following viewpoint. He looks for clues as far back as the Franco-Prussian War, but is especially interested in the EU's absorption first of Greece, Portugal, and Spain—all of which, at one time, were fascist nations—and then, after the fall of the Soviet Union, of eleven communist countries. The EU did the best it could to turn those places into constitutional democracies, but Bisk argues that the disparity of political history and its social symptoms explains the incompatibility of the UK with the rest of Europe.

Historical Comparison

In 1861—72 years after the ratification of the Constitution in 1789—the southern states of the United States exited the American Union. In 2016—70 years after Winston Churchill first called for the establishment of a United States of Europe in 1946—Great Britain exited the European Union.

Both events signified the greatest crises of both amalgamations, threatening the very existence of both. The American crisis triggered humanity's first industrial war and consequent slaughter never equaled by any of America's subsequent wars. This industrialized civil war presaged the greater industrial slaughter and mass means of murder of the 20th century—the two world wars and the Holocaust.

"BREXIT – some historical perspective," by Tsvi Bisk, IEEE, August 30, 2016. Reprinted by Permission. Tsvi Bisk is an Israeli Futurist. His most recent book is The Suicide of the Jews.

The United States emerged from its carnage a much more powerful union—if not yet a more perfect union. From "these united states" (the lower case form customary before the Civil War) it became "The United States" (definite article, upper case).

The United States experienced a "big bang" of industrial, constitutionalist, democratic and cultural progress that transformed it from what had been a relatively backward country before the Civil War into the greatest material and military power in history, as well as the greatest cultural and economic influence on global civilization in the 20th century.

The horrific industrialized slaughter of the 20th century prompted Churchill, in 1946, to call for a United States of Europe in order to prevent another European Civil War, which is what WWI and WWII essentially were (even the Asian theater was characterized, to no small extent, by competing European imperialisms).

The horror of recent history, reinforced by the catastrophic economic conditions of Europe following the war, led to the beginning of a historical process that began in 1949 and evolved into the present day EU. What has been the record of the EU and its antecedents? For the most part, I would claim that it has been overwhelmingly positive.

The most important achievement is that over the past 70 years there have been no wars between France and Germany and thus no European civil wars and consequently no world wars. In the 70 years preceding WWII there were three wars featuring France and Germany: The Franco-Prussian, WWI and WWII. These wars were all related and from a deep historical perspective might be seen as one continuous war with various intermissions, much as the Wars of Religion in the 16th and 17th centuries.

Clemenceau had not forgotten the contempt with which the French were treated by Bismarck after the defeat of the Franco-Prussian war. His bitter resentment led to the vengeful terms of the Versailles Treaty. The German resentment of these vengeful terms was skillfully exploited by Hitler and led directly to WWII.

This vicious cycle was broken after WWII by the formation of the antecedents to the EU reinforced by the Marshall Plan—the greatest example of altruistic enlightened self-interest in history. The formation of this relatively unified western European entity living in peace with itself became the most important grand strategic component of American security policy well into the 21st century.

As such, it became the vital economic complement to NATO in holding the line against Soviet expansion. There may not have been a formal institutional or constitutional link between the two, but it is difficult to deny that these two amalgamations worked hand in hand in countless economic, security and intelligence ways.

In fulfilling this role of economic complement to NATO, the EU raised the economic standard of living of Western Europe to levels rivaling that of North America and the social level of its citizens—in terms of health, welfare and education—to levels unprecedented in human history.

This soft economic and social power successfully undermined the fundamental communist narrative and thus, eventually, made a major contribution to the dissolution of the Soviet empire and the fall of communism in Eastern Europe. So while NATO held the line against the Soviets, the very success of the EU eroded its moral and intellectual pretensions until its ultimate collapse.

As it was eroding Soviet power the EU absorbed three former fascist countries (Greece, Portugal and Spain). The demands of EU membership put them on the road to constitutionalist democracy. After the fall of the Soviet Empire, it absorbed eleven former communist countries, also putting them on the path to constitutionalist democracy.

The present crisis of the EU is in large part a consequence of absorbing these 14 formerly totalitarian countries while their economies, standards of living and political cultures lagged so far behind the 13 very developed countries. The internal migrations towards a better standard of living from the 14 to the 13 were a major contributor to Brexit as well as other populist movements amongst the developed member states.

Yet can anyone seriously deny that the EU fulfilled a monumental historical duty in absorbing these countries. This has been one of the great achievements of recent history—one that only the EU could have accomplished. Because the USA could not have performed this historical task, the EU has shown itself to be not a counterbalance to the USA, but rather a complement to the USA in the spread of constitutionalist democracy.

So, whatever the complaints against the present EU—and they are numerous, substantive and justified—its contribution to human progress and wellbeing is unmatched in history. And even though it is now in deep crisis, this crisis is nowhere near as severe as that of the USA 70 some years after its inception.

The Special Case of England

So what motivated Great Britain towards Brexit? I suggest that Britain's problem with the EU has more profound roots than just current annoyance with the petty tyrannies of a supercilious EU bureaucracy (as real and justified as those are). It is just as much a feeling that "their England" is no longer English but a "mixed multitude"—an aggregate of alien sub-cultures with no real center, or emotional anchor, or sense of place or meaningful connection to traditional English political, cultural and social traditions.

England and continental Europe have always had a difficult relationship. The English political tradition is different from the continental political tradition. This difference originates in the Magna Carta, which affirmed that the King did not have absolute power but must adhere to the Common Law of the land. No one was above the law, and the law certainly did not reside in the very person of the monarch as France's Louise 14th indicated when he famously said "the State is Me." This is the political/cultural/social genome that put England on the path to constitutionalism, just as all the continental states (with the exception of the Netherlands) were on the path to absolutism.

English political culture has evolved in such a way as to put the individual in the center while continental Europe's political culture has evolved in such a way as to put the State in the center. Nothing characterizes this more than the parliamentary practice of "surgeries" in which MPs receive constituents one-on-one to hear their complaints. Amazingly, even in the midst of the Brexit campaign, PM Cameron took time out to hold periodic surgeries, meeting with individuals from his parliamentary constituency.

England's paramount political philosopher was John Locke, who, in his Two Treatises on Government, managed to encapsulate the English political temperament that stemmed from the Magna Carta, the Three Summonses to Parliament, The Petition of Right and finally the English Bill of Rights (the precursor of the American Constitution). Indeed, American political culture could justifiably be described as "England 2.0."

Continental political thinking, on the other hand, has been dominated by Hegel and Rousseau. The preeminence of the State and the state bureaucracy characterizes much of what Hegel wrote. Rousseau celebrated "the general will"—an open invitation to Majoritarian Democracy, the mother of Totalitarian Democracy, which is sometimes called Fascism.

The European states were, in effect, created top-down by the state bureaucracy. The English state, on the other hand, was created incrementally bottom-up—i.e. the development of the English "state" and English constitutionality are entwined. This is what differentiates the American Revolution from the French Revolution. The American Revolution was but another iteration of English constitutional development (defending their "rights as Englishmen"), while the French Revolution was but another iteration of French absolutism. While the French celebrated the general will, the American founding fathers rejected the tyranny of the majority that is inherent in Majoritarian Democracy.

This distinction bears the essence of the disconnect between Britain and the EU. The institutions of the EU reflect the bureaucratic and majoritarian political tradition of Germany and France rather than the individualistic Anglo Saxon tradition.

Language has much to do with the different perspectives. In English it is much easier to love one's country while hating the "state" (Americans are very good at this). In Europe, especially Germany, it is almost impossible to do so. Patriotism is intrinsically involved with loyalty to the state that guarantees national and personal liberty. In the Anglo-Saxon world it is involved with loyalty to certain constitutionalist principles that limit the power of the state vis-à-vis the individual citizen.

The "centrality of the State" mindset that characterizes European bureaucrats leads of necessity to an absolutist turn of mind: a one- size-fits-all mentality that has little tolerance for national idiosyncrasies. Ironically, that same European attitude that professes to celebrate multiculturalism, in fact practices monoculturalism in its bureaucratic traditions. They made absolutely no allowances for English exceptionalism, an exceptionalism that has almost 1,000 years of tradition.

This is why the English never felt comfortable with the EU and why the petty annoyances of an arrogant and condescending bureaucracy in Brussels drove them to distraction more than other European countries.

VIEWPOINT 7

Brexit and "the Other"

Marie-Pierre Moreau

"The association of the Leave voter with (white, working-class, middle age) femininity is only one of several narratives which have emerged during the referendum, but it is one of particular significance," says RISE Research Centre director Marie-Pierre Moreau in this viewpoint. Brexit, she believes, was an exercise in othering in order to reassert "social, gender, race, national, and other divides." Brexit is thus best understood not as a "working-class revolt" but as the effort of a privileged few (affluent, white men) to safeguard their relevance and preserve their social and political power. Moreau is also the Reader in Sociology of Education at the University of Roehampton.

Introduction

Over the last week, members of GEA's executive committee have been sharing their views on Donald Trump's election success; Andrea Peto started by examining how Trump's win was a boost for illiberial regimes in Europe. Jessica Ringrose and Victoria Showunmi then considered how to call out Trump pedagogy by turning the 2016 USA election into a teachable moment. Finally, we saw a piece by Sally Campbell Galman that reinforced the phrase "the personal is political" as she articulated what the win meant on an intimate level with her post, "We ain't whupped yet: Memo from America 11/10." Today, exec member, Marie-Pierre Moreau shares her views on Brexit and the politics of othering.

Here at GEA we are proud that our executive committee are dedicated to sharing good practice and their views on life

"Brexit and The Rise of Right-Wing Populism: a Politics of Othering," by Dr. Marie-Pierre Moreau, Gender and Education, November 16, 2016. Reprinted by Permission.

events; this series has been popular with readers and we have enjoyed reading your comments on Twitter, Facebook and in the comments section of the posts. We are also proud of the fact that we offer writing opportunities to readers—if you would like to share your views on Trump's election, Brexit or any other issue, please contact us!

Brexit and The Rise of Right-Wing Populism: a Politics of Othering

When David Cameron promised, during the 2015 general election campaign, to hold a referendum on the EU, very few would have anticipated that his pledge would result in months of intensive campaigning during which politicians would turn against each other in the harshest imaginable ways. Nor was it anticipated that Leave/Remain would become the new significant political divider that it is. In a country which prizes itself for being inclusive and where items printed with "keep calm and carry on" sell like hot cakes, the level of turmoil associated with the referendum has been unusual in recent history.

On a personal level, the shocking realisation that 52% of voters expressed a preference for the UK leaving the EU has been painful, especially given the racist undertones of the campaign. Having felt welcome in this country for many years, I experienced feelings of betrayal and powerlessness, with the latter exacerbated by the fact that I could not vote. Yet I was not so prepared for the emotional turmoil that my British friends and colleagues went through (none of them, from their own admission, had voted Leave). They were full of anger, sadness, but also shame. This was not the future they envisaged for themselves, nor for their children. They identified with being the victim and with being the culprit—some even apologised to me, as if they bore some form of responsibility in what had just happened.

So when I woke up after just about three hours of interrupted sleep on Friday 24 June, there were still two camps, except now the one I was not part of had won. Months of debate had unleashed racism and xenophobia. This, of course, was not new. We know, thanks to a wealth of research on the topic, that in the UK, as in many other countries, ethnic and religious minorities have been subjected to considerable levels of racism and hatred for decades. If anything, this has been exacerbated by the referendum campaign. However, with the referendum, a new figure of hatred has been revealed: that of the "European" migrant. Of course, this too is not completely new. German and French people, for example, are regularly subjected to stereotyping and mockeries. Irish and, in the more recent period, Polish and other Eastern European migrants have attracted some particularly negative feelings. During the referendum and in the days that followed it, this form of racism seemed to have intensified.

Anecdotes of daily micro-aggressions were shared with European friends. Tabloids, in favour of the Leave campaign, published abusive articles about European migrants. "Leave the EU/No more Polish vermin" leaflets were delivered in several towns across the UK; xenophobic graffiti were sprayed outside a Polish cultural centre; European citizens suffered extreme abuse, including one instance of a racially motivated killing. This political turmoil culminated with the death of Jo Cox, a Labour MP in favour of Remain, murdered by a member of her constituency as he shouted "Britain First." The political rhetoric of the Leave camp and of many among the new post-referendum Government became increasingly tainted by the melancholic fantasies of a lost empire (Cain, 2016). European migrants are ostracised in increasingly overt ways and a politics of othering is at play. While we are soon to be "out'" racism is definitely "in,'" and Europhobia has joined in on a new scale. This of course finds an unfortunate echo across the Atlantic, as the US presidential campaign and its aftermaths have been tainted by considerable levels of xenophobia, misogyny, transphobia and ableism, ending with a victory of a man whose political rhetoric and personal life resonate with each other when it comes to these matters.

But, as I quickly came to realise, something else had happened. This process of othering had now extended to a range of groups "suspected" to have voted Leave en masse. On BBC Newsnight, a few days after the referendum, a journalist interviewed four voters. On the left, two Leave voters: both women from Boston, Lincolnshire, middle-aged, White British and working-class. On the right, two Remain voters: both young men from Lambeth, London, one White British, the other British Asian, one a lawyer, the other a student, middle-class. Asked why she voted Leave, one of the participants mentioned the many "European EU workers"' living in her town who "can't even say 'hello' in English." On the other side, the two Remain voters listened politely. While the racists words used by the Leave supporters were violent, so was the media mise en scène, contrasting the confused, provincial, female, White, middle-aged, working-class narrative of the Leave voter with those of their articulate, confident, young, cosmopolitan, male, middle-class Remain counterpart. Their bodies became the signifiers of class, gender and race, with one group embodying bigotry and "chavism," the other modernity and the charme discret de la bourgeoisie-in other words, privilege. The symbolic violence of this scene has stayed with me. With it came the realisation that "Brexit" was about much more than the othering of (a group of highly diverse) European migrants.

What played out in this scene and in many others which would be repeated ad libitum and ad nauseam by the media in the following days was the awakening and possibly strengthening of divisions which have long been present in British and other Western societies. The association of the Leave voter with (White, working-class, middle-age) femininity is only one of several narratives which have emerged during the referendum, but it is one of particular significance. The scene I recalled above fits the post-industrial deficit discourse of the working-class as "chavs" discussed by Owen Jones in his eponymous book. Although exit polls show a positive correlation between being working-class and voting Leave, gender parity prevailed when it comes to political allegiances. Fifty-two percent of female voters voted in favour of Brexit, that is exactly the same percentage as men (unfortunately, more intersectional data are hard to come by). However, as for class, the scene fits a narrative that goes back a long way and constructs women as irrational and politically incompetent. Those who take a political stance are often demonised, as in the case of Hillary Clinton and of Gina Miller, when they are not simply invisible and silenced, as has happened to female politicians during the UK referendum campaign.

Let us remind ourselves that in the UK women gained the right to vote in 1928 as a result of the Equal Franchise Act (although some women were able to vote from 1918). Today, women represent less than 30% of Members of Parliament. They face incredible barriers and will frequently lose elections against less experienced and less competent male candidates, a point strikingly illustrated by the recent US elections. Theresa May and, before her, Margaret Thatcher are exceptions in an incredibly male-dominated environment and in many ways are highly privileged. There is also an irony of constructing working-class women as the abject figure of the Leave workers. The EU has invested some considerable resources in tackling gender inequality and social exclusion. Working-class women are among the most likely to be affected by the economical uncertainties associated with Brexit, with limited impact on the likes of Boris Johnson and Nigel Farage.

Concluding this piece on a hopeful note would have proved to be a challenge, if it had not been for my spell checker coming to the rescue and changing the subtitle of this piece into the politics of "bothering." After all, as long as we bother, we remain political animals who, I am naïve enough to think, care about the public good and individual rights. When young voters have been blamed, rightly or wrongly, for their political apathy, the referendum campaign and subsequent turmoil may help to bring divides to the fore and provoke the political awakening which we needed. A consequence of the social segregation and territorialisation of inequalities is that, like many, I have yet to meet somebody who has voted Leave (an admission which I am sure would be complicated by the fact that I am after all a European migrant with a distinctive foreign accent). Let us recall here that voters based in London and Scotland overwhelmingly voted for Remain and so did 3 out of 4 voters in the town where I live. Segregation facilitates the demonisation of those who are 'not like us'. Thus, there is a real onus on all of us to move away from the simplistic, divisive fantasies of 'social abjection' (Tyler, 2016) revealed by the referendum and draw on critical and intersectional perspectives.

We also need to ask who benefits from a politics of othering which reasserts social, gender, race, national and other divides. While Brexit has been sold as a victory for the working-class, we should not forget that the leaders of the Leave camp are by a huge majority wealthy, privately educated White men. In many ways, the rise of right-wing populisms in the UK, the US and elsewhere, can be interpreted as a backlash aiming to maintain the privileges associated with being part of these groups. So while we should not encourage the emergence of a new figure of hatred, we need to challenge the racist, misogynistic, classist and nationalist rhetoric of Brexit and of the US elections that plays certain groups against each other. Academics can play a key role in this, although this is a difficult task at a time when universities and workers of the knowledge economy are derided. Yet, in the face of hatred, we must continue to engage with social justice issues through our ongoing scholarship, our contribution to national, international and transnational public debates and our pedagogical practices. We owe it to those with less privilege and we are certainly not short of research material.

Chapter 2

Perspectives, Controversies, and Debates

Preface

In the weeks after the referendum, one line was repeated throughout the United Kingdom: Brexit means Brexit. But, really, what does that mean? As the UK and EU steel themselves for an unwinding that could well take a decade—the former sure-fire, the latter spurned and obdurate—so much is left unsolved. In this chapter, you'll encounter a range of opinions that will illuminate your understanding of Brexit's implications.

To begin with, an illustrious panel of economists take on two key questions: What will Brexit do to the UK's short-term growth, and what will it mean for long-term financial prospects? Elsewhere, writers wonder whether Brexit will undermine the EU, clog British courts, mire the nation in deceitful cloud cover, elicit honest conversations about race and xenophobia, or inspire a new political movement.

You will see, in the following pages, that the inextricable link between economic trends and social realities creates political outcomes. One lively voice on this subject is George Monboit, who calls Brexit "the eruption of an internal wound, inflicted over many years by an economic oligarchy on the poor and the forgotten."

The following voices are thoughtful, scholarly, and impassioned. Above all, they reveal the tangle of social, economic, and political transformations to which Brexit has given rise.

Viewpoint 1

It's Unanimous: Brexit Will Stymie Growth

Chris Giles and Emily Cadman

In 2016, before the referendum vote, the Financial Times *asked more than 100 economists whether Brexit would help or hurt the UK's prospects of short-term growth. None thought Brexit would be good for growth. What's more, nearly three-quarters of those surveyed felt Brexit would also "damage the [UK's] medium-term outlook." The following viewpoint by* Financial Times *writers Giles and Cadman presents a large sample of those economists' thoughts on the fiscal implications of Brexit as they peer at an uncertain future.*

There are few issues that unite UK economists but Brexit is one of them: they overwhelmingly believe leaving the EU is bad for the country's economic prospects.

In the FT's annual poll of more than 100 leading thinkers, not one thought a vote for Brexit would enhance UK growth in 2016.

Almost three-quarters thought leaving the EU would damage the country's medium-term outlook, nine times more than the 8 per cent who thought the country would benefit from leaving. Less than 18 per cent thought it would make little difference.

One of the greatest reasons for economists fearing a vote to leave is that it would spark huge uncertainty, which stops companies investing and households spending, harming growth.

Adam Posen, president of the Peterson Institute for International Economics said the "huge self-inflicted wound" of a vote for Brexit

"Economists' forecasts: Brexit would damage growth," by Chris Giles and Emily Cadman, *Financial Times* Ltd, January 03, 2016. Used under licence from the Financial Times.

"changes my views about 2016 and the medium term drastically for the worse. Business investment will dry up rapidly."

Many feared the consequences for financial markets would be severe. Don Smith, deputy chief investment officer at Brown Shipley, said: "The uncertainty generated by a decision to leave the EU would undoubtedly be damaging for sterling assets across the board and, indeed, the value of sterling on foreign exchanges. Consumer confidence would be lower, business confidence and investment intentions would also very likely be negatively impacted."

Most of the 36 per cent of economists saying there would be little impact in 2016 came to that view because they thought a vote would come too late to materially affect the year's economic data.

Gavyn Davies, Chairman of Fulcrum Asset Management, was typical in saying, "the referendum will not make any major difference to 2016 views. However, a No vote would lead to a sharp drop in growth in 2017, due to political uncertainty, worries about Scotland's status inside the UK, an upheaval in the financial services industry, and a major drop in inward capital flows into the UK."

If the British electorate votes to leave the EU in 2016, how would that change your views about a) the prospects for next year b) the medium term

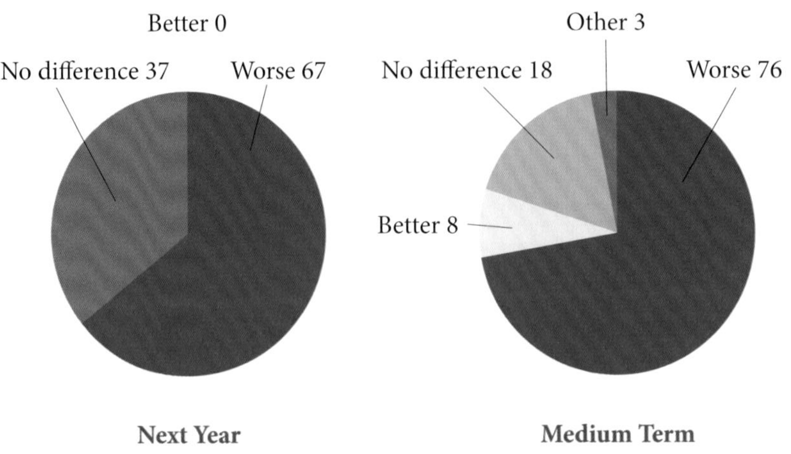

Source: FT Survey

Further into the future, where opinion was even more strongly opposed to leaving the EU, concerns were centred on the risk that many international companies would no longer choose Britain as a base for their European operations and that the suggested benefits of new trading relations with emerging economies were something of a mirage.

John van Reenen, director of the Centre for Economic Performance, said: "In addition to a loss of trade there will be a loss of foreign investment and less inward migration from highly talented Europeans who have aided UK growth. The idea that we'll be able to strike lots of new free trade deals with other countries being free from EU is fantasy, as is the idea that there will be some bonfire of red tape that lights up UK growth."

Stephen King, adviser to HSBC, noted that Britain's economy had "flourished" in the EU. "Footballers that leave clubs where they have done well have sometimes underperformed thereafter: just think of Fernando Torres at Liverpool and then at Chelsea. Could the UK be heading the same way?" he asked.

Others worried that new freedoms to set regulations might harm competitiveness and growth. Ricardo Reis, professor of economics at London School of Economics, said that while leaving "could allow for some policy improvements, it would also open the way for a whole list of dreadful policies regarding trade, immigration, and industrial policy that membership in the EU now precludes".

The small minority who thought the UK would benefit from an exit tended to think that any freedoms would be used to foster a more prosperous society, rejecting Prof Reis's concerns.

Gerard Lyons, economic adviser to Boris Johnson, mayor of London, said the best outcome was being a member of a "truly reformed" EU, but if that was not possible, "the choice may be a stark one, between the UK being in an EU that is inward looking [and] insular, as the EU's share of the world economy shrinks, or outside, trading with the whole world including Europe, negotiating our own, better suited, trade deals with a focus on what the UK is good at".

If the British electorate vote to leave the EU in 2016, how would that: a) change your views about prospects for next year? b) change your views about medium-term prospects?

Anonymous

In the short run it won't make any difference, not least because we won't be sure what it means In the medium term it will, not least because people won't know what it means. Hard to expect Nissan to invest in Sunderland when they don't know what Brexit means, when it will happen, etc.

Anonymous

It would dampen my views for 2016 but not alter those for the medium term. Indeed, it might marginally improve the longer-term outlook. The short term would inevitably see considerable uncertainty—about the reaction of the Scots, the terms of an exit and the consequences particularly for financial services trade. But in the longer term, the exit of the UK would probably not make a great difference to the direction and scale of UK trade, especially with Germany, which would want Britain to remain a market open to its exports.

Anonymous

At a high level it is difficult to see any big positive impacts for the UK economy from a vote to leave the EU, while it is easy to see plenty of potential negative impacts. The immediate impact next year would most likely come through a sharp increase in business uncertainty, delayed investment and potentially currency volatility. Medium term prospects would depend crucially on the type of settlement that was negotiated after a vote for exit but it is hard to imagine any large medium term upsides.

Anonymous

The main problem with Brexit is that, if it were to occur, no one would have the slightest idea about how our revised relationship with the EU would be arranged. The uncertainty would be intense, and the short-term effects significantly adverse. I have little doubt that if the UK were to leave the EU, we could cope relatively well on our own in the longer term, but it would cast a considerable pall over the immediate subsequent two years, or so. If we look longer at a ten year horizon, it is not clear to me whether the longer-term effect would be good or bad.

Anonymous

The referendum itself will lift uncertainty and bear down on asset prices and growth.

Brexit means more than exiting EU—it also means several years of domestic political uncertainty, the prospect of a further Scottish referendum and uncertain international trade and investment relations. Even if the long-term outcome is only marginally worse than under continued membership, the loss of output and the negative impact on asset prices could stretch for years.

Anonymous

Brexit would probably trigger weakness in sterling and bring forward interest rate increases. Growth will be weaker as the UK will be seen as a less attractive place to locate a business. Investment and productivity growth would be weaker as a result.

Howard Archer, Chief European & UK Economist, IHS Global Insight

It would cause us to lower our GDP growth forecast for 2016 and highly likely for 2017 as well. Even if you believe the UK would actually be better off outside the EU in the long-run, there will be substantial uncertainty for some time in the aftermath of the decision to leave and this will likely hit both domestic and foreign investment in the UK. It could also undermine investor confidence in UK assets, at least for a while. For example, it will take time to establish the parameters of the UK's relationship with the EU on trade and access to single market, and it will also take time to establish any trade agreements with other regions.

There is also likely to be more of a dampening impact on UK economic activity through heightened uncertainty, in the run-up to the referendum if the opinion polls start regularly showing the Brexit side ahead.(not that the opinion polls have a particularly good record recently in the UK!)

It is impossible to really say at this stage how we would change our views for the medium-term outlook for the UK economy at this stage. There are just too many uncertainties.

Much depends on the extent of the trade agreements that the UK reaches after Brexit—not only with the EU but also with other regions/countries. Other important factors include how much the UK is affected by non-trade barriers when exporting to the EU, the amount of deregulation that is undertaken in the UK, what immigration policy is followed, how the City of London's role as a dominant financial centre and foreign direct investment into the UK are affected. There are also questions as to whether UK economic dynamism could be seriously undermined—or alternatively unlocked—which is not easy to capture in any economic cost-benefit analysis of Brexit.

There is little doubt that the greater and more comprehensive the trade agreements that the UK comes to after Brexit—both with the EU and with other regions/countries—the better (or less badly) the UK is likely to fare after Brexit. But even here there are uncertainties. One concern, for example, is that by engaging in more trade agreements with countries/regions outside the EU, UK companies could be increasingly exposed to competition in their domestic market from very low-cost companies. If this did happen, a key question would be how UK companies responded to this increased competition and if it helped UK economic dynamism by encouraging innovation. If UK companies failed to respond, there would be the risk that it could lead to some manufacturing sectors suffering a serious hollowing out. This would threaten to outweigh any wider benefits to the UK economy coming from cheaper imported goods

Melanie Baker, Jacob Nell, Morgan Stanley

A vote to leave could see the UK flirting with recession by late 2016. Political and economic uncertainty, reflected in market volatility (especially for FX and equities), would be followed by a sharp slowdown in domestic growth, with investment particularly affected. Medium term, we think that a UK exit would imply slower potential growth—lower migration inflows and lower productivity growth as a result of lower capital inflows.

Kate Barker, former MPC member

It would not change my views for next year. And I'm not sure how much it would affect long-term prospects—though medium-term ones would be worse as the economy would enter an adjustment period due to the impact on different sectors. Much would depend on the trade negotiations as an 'out' and on the reaction of the Cit—the latter seems likely to be a key negative.

Nicholas Barr, Professor of Public Economics, LSE

(a) worse
(b) much worse

Ray Barrell, Professor, Brunel University and VA Research

The increase in uncertainty engendered by the possibility of UK exit from the UK has been one of the main factors holding back investment and growth in the UK in the last few years. If the probability of exit rises then investment plans are likely to be scaled back further, and growth will weaken in 2016. Conversely a positive outcome, with the UK staying in the EU, would provide an immediate boost to growth as uncertainty would be reduced and the medium term negative impacts of exit would be absent.

b) The positive impacts of EU membership on growth are well documented, and in addition output is probably three per cent higher than it would otherwise have been given the Single

Market Programme and associated policies that have strengthened competition in the UK. Many businesses in the UK might prefer a less competitive, more profit friendly, environment, and that is why they may favour exit, albeit at a cost to others. One of the major channels of the positive influence of the EU on the UK has been Foreign Direct Investment. The impacts of exit on FDI are statistically difficult to ascertain, but it is clear that US and Japanese firms have seen the UK as a production base for the whole of Europe, and the potential for barriers to trade will reduce their desire to produce in the UK. Exit from the UK will potentially reduce UK output by two to three per cent in the medium term as compared to where it would otherwise have been, and hence potential growth is likely to fall by a quarter of a per cent for a decade, reversing the gains we have made in the last twenty years. Membership has been unambiguously beneficial, with the negative effects of an expensive agricultural protection regime having largely disappeared with reform and the decline in its share of output. It is also unlikely that the EU will be willing to extend all the benefits of membership to a country that has chosen to exit an ever closer union. Hence exit will have costs, but remains a political as well as economic decision.

Richard Barwell, Senior Economist, BNP Paribas

It's hard to reach a definitive conclusion about what an out vote really means in the medium term until we know the details of our post-exit settlement with Europe—in particular, the terms on which our companies will gain access to European markets—and for that matter, the ramifications of that deal for the political settlement within the United Kingdom. I struggle to see how that uncertainty could be rapidly resolved so in the short run, the safe bet is that the significant and sustained spike in uncertainty will weigh on growth. To the extent that macroeconomists understand investment at all, we think that this kind of shock to uncertainty will raise the hurdle rate on major investment projects leading companies to delay spending. No doubt the public will have been repeatedly told in the run-up to the vote that millions of jobs depend on our continued membership of the European Union so there would likely be some impact on consumer confidence and consumer spending too.

Charles Bean, Professor of Economics, London School of Economics

Brexit—actual or expected—may encourage some businesses to postpone (or even cancel) planned investment. Were the UK to decide to leave, renegotiation of the terms of our relationship with the EU would probably take several years to achieve and may well prove contentious with other member states. The continuing uncertainty surrounding the terms of access of UK firms to the EU market mean that this dampening effect on investment could be expected to last for several years.

Andrew Benito, Goldman Sachs, Senior European Economist

The UK's in/out referendum on continued membership of the EU will donate the year ahead. Our view that the UK will vote to retain its EU membership is based on the public deciding to prioritise its economic interests and avoid a lengthy period of elevated uncertainty that would follow an exit. We believe a vote to leave the EU would weaken the outlook for activity significantly.

In the event of an EU exit, foreign investors—currently happy to finance a sizeable current account deficit and roll over large gross external liabilities of the UK on the grounds that the finances an economy growing at trend—would likely reassess those views. Credit conditions would tighten as bank funding costs rise and spending plans would be disrupted.

The growth impact in the longer-term would depend on how exit affected trend productivity growth and expansion of the labour force. Were it to happen, a vote to leave the EU would presumably be motivated partly by wishing to reduce levels of immigration, suggesting these medium-term effects would also be negative.

Nick Bosanquet, Professor, Imperial

Would not impact 2016–17—but some medium terms effects on business confidence. Knock on effects for political stability would be more important than Euro trade effects.

Ryan Bourne, Head of public policy, Institute of Economic Affairs

a) Voting to leave would obviously create a degree of uncertainty in the immediate two years after we presumably have triggered Article 50, particularly if it became unclear whether a free-trade agreement would not be negotiated in this time period. But much of this risk is surely already priced in given the heavily fluctuating polling on this issue. I guess it really depends on how the debate shapes up and subsequently what "out" would mean and how this affected investment decisions. There's no reason per se that voting to leave would change prospects, particularly if we transition to out by remaining in the single market to begin, but if it became clear that voting to leave was perceived as a mandate merely to clamp down on migration, that could be more problematic.

b) Looking at countries inside and outside, it's clear that EU membership is neither a necessary or sufficient condition for good economic growth—domestic policy is far more important. The EU question is largely a political question about where sovereignty should reside. But there seems little benefit for the UK of some of the harmonisation outlined for the near future in the Five Presidents' report—so I fully expect that provided domestic policy remains sensible and economically liberal and a mutually beneficial free trade is agreed, the medium-term prospects associated with being outside would improve relative to remaining in.

Francis Breedon, Professor, QMUL

Little in the short or long run. Hard to find evidence that EU membership has a significant growth effect (though balance of evidence suggests that exit would have a small negative impact).

Annika Breidthardt, European Commission
We do not speculate on hypothetical questions.

George Buckley, Chief UK Economist, Deutsche Bank
a) Next year: Irrespective of the outcome, the uncertainty surrounding the referendum may begin to impact business investment in advance of the vote. After all, the UK is the biggest recipient of inward investment anywhere outside of the US. It would not be surprising to hear that some overseas firms end up postponing—or worse, diverting to other countries—inward direct investment in advance of the referendum.

b) In the medium-term there are sizeable economic risks associated with exit. Much would depend on what sort of deal the UK could broker with the EU. On the one hand, the EU has a vested interested to maintain good trade links and offer a preferential deal. On the other, they might be keen to avoid exit-contagion by being less generous in post-EU-exit trade negotiations. We would expect investment to suffer the most from an exit (particularly in the event of ratings downgrades), with the impact on growth being only partly offset by a fall in the currency.

Alan Budd, former MPC member
Unless the referendum is held early in the year, uncertainty relating to the referendum will be more important than the vote itself. Uncertainty relates both to the result of the vote and to the consequences of a vote to leave. Both sources of uncertainty are likely to harm investment spending in the short and medium term.

Willem Buiter, Citigroup, Global Chief Economist
Should Brexit occur, the economic impact of a divorce from the EU would be dramatic. The rest of the EU would drive a very hard bargain with the UK ("pour decourager les autres"); the City would lose most euro-related business. FDI into the UK would collapse. Deep recession and a financial crisis are inevitable. In addition, Brexit would be followed promptly by the break-up of the UK: Scotland, Wales and Northern Ireland leave the UK and

join the EU; I would hope that Greater London—the region inside the M25—would leave England and join the EU. Even if England stays intact.

Jagjit Chadha, Professor of Economics, University of Kent

Given that there is a commitment to have a referendum, it is a good idea to have it earlier rather than later because a looming referendum feeds uncertainty. A vote to leave the EU may not impact much on growth in 2016, as many plans have already been formulated but would clearly involve a considerable reorientation of the economy, which is likely to be costly in the short run. The medium and long term prospects depend on access to the free trade blocs that make up the structure of world trade and the impact on financial and other services, which are not clear to me.

Alan Clarke, Economist, Scotiabank

Just by announcing the date of the referendum is likely to have an impact on the data. The general election campaign saw employment growth stall as firms were fearful of a messy coalition or non-business friendly government (that soon reversed after the election result). I would envisage a re-run of this (potentially more severe) once the date of the EU referendum is known—with hiring intentions and investment intentions particularly hit in the months ahead of the vote. I would also expect the GBP exchange rate to weaken somewhat as the vote approaches, which may help inflation to firm a little. If the UK were to vote to leave the EU, I would envisage investors would adopt a "risk-off" stance—with gilt yields rising and the GBP exchange rate weakening. Weaker investment would be the most likely dampener on growth in the first instance, though consumption could also suffer if hiring stalls or consumer confidence suffers. Uncertainty is the enemy for sentiment—this kind of event doesn't happen very often.

Over the medium term, the prospects for the UK could depend on the response of our trading partners within the Eurozone. The UK imports far more goods from the Eurozone than it exports in the other direction. Hence the EU has a lot to lose if traditional trading links become severed. As a result, there is good reason for the EU to maintain trade links with the UK outside of the EU. The majority of UK services exports go outside of the EU, which suggests that this sector is less vulnerable to a fractious divorce. So while going it alone is a leap of faith into the unknown, there are some reasons to believe that it need not be the disaster that some of the scare stories may lead us to believe.

David Cobham, Professor of economics, Heriot-Watt University

It won't make much difference to real income (though it will affect financial markets) in 2016, but it will have strong and lasting negative effects over the medium and long term.

Aengus Collins, Country Forecast Director, The Economist Intelligence Unit

It's probably worth noting at the outset that our view at The EIU is that the electorate will vote narrowly to stay in the EU, with the pull of the status quo ultimately overcoming the push of rising public disaffection, not just with Brussels but with UK migration policy too. Turning to the question's hypothetical "no" vote, the EIU isn't expecting the Brexit referendum to be held before late 2016, so a vote to leave would not have a material impact on our projections for next year.

The medium-term impact would be much more significant. It would be more political than economic: party-political stability and government effectiveness would suffer in the wake of so direct a public rejection of mainstream political consensus. That political backdrop is an important, but often overlooked, part of any assessment of the economic impact of a "no" vote. The uncertainty unleashed by a vote for Brexit would hit consumer confidence and spending in the relatively short term, while a drop-off in business investment would exacerbate existing concerns about the economy's medium-term prospects.

Diane Coyle, Professor of economics, University of Manchester
What we do know is that the uncertainty will hit consumer and institutional confidence, which means a drop in consumer spending and investment. There are so many unknowns it is hard to gauge the extent of the fallout. Would it hurt the City of London as a financial centre, would the rest of Europe (unofficially) boycott the UK, would sterling be more volatile?

What about the EU itself? The UK is the third-biggest economy and it could trigger a crisis in Europe, which wouldn't be good for the UK either.

In the medium term, I am more optimistic. The UK is a small, open, globalised economy and the growing areas of the world are outside Europe.

Howard Davies, RBB, Chairman
I doubt if a Brexit referendum can be mounted in time to affect the economy next year. But a "leave" vote would probably dampen investment and growth in the medium term, at least until the terms of a new deal with the EU became clear.

Gavyn Davies, Chairman, Fulcrum Asset Management
The referendum will not make any major difference to 2016 views. However, a no vote would lead to a sharp drop in growth in 2017, due to political uncertainty, worries about Scotland's status inside the UK, an upheaval in the financial services industry, and a major drop in inward capital flows into the UK.

Panicos Demetriades, Professor of Financial Economics, Ex-Governor of Central Bank of Cyprus and member of the Governing Council of the ECB, University of Leicester
There is no doubt that Brexit is a factor that will weigh heavily on the prospects of the U.K. economy and beyond. Besides the obvious barriers to trade and impediments to capital flows it is likely to create, it may unleash political and economic uncertainty relating to the future of the European project that could have deleterious economic consequences in the whole of Europe. Although the vote

itself is unlikely to have much of an impact in 2016, it will almost certainly affect the medium term prospects of the U.K. economy.

Wouter Den Haan, professor of economics, London School of Economics
I would be more pessimistic about the UKs prospects at any horizon if it would leave the EU, unless the EU is hit by a major calamity such as a complete collapse because of the refugee crisis.

Michael Devereux, Professor, Oxford university
Brexit could only have a negative effect on the UK economy—for example, the UK would be less attractive as a business location. But I have no idea about the magnitude of the effect.

I'd say the downside could happen quickly—and even as it is debated since it increases uncertainty.

Peter Dixon, Economist, Commerzbank
(a) Not very much. There might be something of an uncertainty shock but since the rules point to business as usual until the formal exit negotiations have concluded, I would not envisage changing my 2016 forecasts by much;

(b) We are in more uncertain territory here. The empirical literature suggests a hit to GDP of anywhere between 0% and 3% over the medium-term. If we broadly split the difference, and call it 2% over 10 years, this would knock almost 0.25 percentage points off annual growth in the decade following Brexit. If the transition period is shorter (longer) the annual growth cost is higher (lower). But this is more than just about measuring growth. Relationships with a spurned EU would inevitably change; if we turn our back on our economic and political allies, we are operating in a world of much greater uncertainty and I would be much less optimistic about our economic future.

Charles Dumas, Director, Lombard Street Research
Not very much on either account. The key thing in Europe is whether a country is in the euro or not—and Britain, fortunately, is not.

Colin Ellis, Birmingham University, Visiting Fellow
In the event of a vote for exit, I think prospects for next year would be a little weaker, and indeed over the medium term (obviously the latter accumulates more for investment/capital deepening/potential supply). However, I see this as more of a levels shock—albeit spread out a lot—than permanently hitting potential growth. I really don't see strong benefits from exit; by most objective measures, we already have very liberalised product and labour markets, and I don't buy some of the numbers that pass for orthodoxy from the likes of the OECD on benefits from structural reforms. But we clearly could survive outside; it wouldn't be the end of the world.

Ultimately, questions like EU membership—or Scottish independence—should always be about much more than the economics. But inaccurate and highly uncertain numbers get bandied around so much, they may end up (further) damaging the profession, insofar as we have any credibility left.

Martin Ellison, Professor of Economics, University of Oxford
The referendum itself will introduce a lot of uncertainty, with likely negative effects on interest rates and sterling through elevated risk premia. Should the vote go in favour of Brexit, the level of uncertainty is likely to shoot through the roof—the future of the UK outside of the EU is surrounded by Knightian uncertainties, the "unknown unknowns" made famous by Donald Rumsfeld. Is it possible for a country to leave the EU is an orderly fashion? How will financial markets react? The UK will obviously survive outside of the EU—life will go on—but it is difficult to see what form it will take and to believe that the process of exiting will not harm short and medium term prospects.

Andrew Goodwin, Lead UK Economist, Oxford Economics

a) I think the effect would be noticeable though it wouldn't be a game changer. Inevitably there will be a period of heightened uncertainty which will be bad news for investment

b) This really depends upon what a post-Brexit UK is destined to look like—the absence thus far of any clear vision for a post-Brexit UK is, in my opinion, one of the biggest failings of the groups campaigning to leave. If the UK is to be a "Norway," ie it remains in the EEA, then the chances are that not a lot will change. But at the other end of the spectrum, if the UK fails to agree a free-trade agreement with the EU then the impact on UK medium-term growth prospects would be more serious.

Jonathan Haskel, Professor of Economics, Imperial College Business School

Leaving the EU would likely cause investment to fall due to raised uncertainty and a fall off in FDI investment. But (measured) investment is very low anyway, having recovered only somewhat from the 2008 recession, so I'd expect a fall in GDP and growth, but not as dramatic as it would be if we were in a substantial investment-led boom.

John Hawksworth, Chief Economist, PwC

The referendum itself is a source of uncertainty for business, but probably relatively marginal in terms of macroeconomic prospects for 2016. If the UK were to vote to leave the EU, whether in 2016 or later, this would lead to a prolonged period of uncertainty as to the exact terms of exit and the impact on different industry sectors, but it is very difficult to quantify these effects with any precision.

Neville Hill, Credit Suisse

In the medium-term we'd see the UK's departure from the EU as being negative for demand—a material hit to exports of services and well as goods—and supply—the UK has benefited from immigration of a labour supply that has largely complemented the domestic working population. So materially negative for GDP and the UK's standard of living.

The risk is that worsening in living standards is delivered in advance by a sharp correction downwards in the value of sterling. A vote to leave the EU could well be the catalytic event that turns the UK's current account deficit from "something to worry about" to "a problem". Given the clear economic risks above, markets would likely demand a considerably higher risk premium the huge capital inflows required to finance that deficit. That'd mean a sharp fall in sterling and the price of UK assets. The UK would then be faced with a noxious cocktail of depressed business confidence; tightening financial conditions; higher inflation (thanks to sterling's drop) falling real wages and monetary policy tightening to offset that higher inflation. In short, a cocktail sufficient to derail the recent solid performance of the UK economy and, possibly, push it into recession.

Brian Hilliard, Société Générale, Chief UK Economist

It would lead me to lower my forecasts because the heightened uncertainty would hurt business and possibly consumer confidence, once the potential consequences had sunk in. Lower growth and thus a lower interest rate profile than in our base case of gentle increases from Q4 16.

Lee Hopley, Chief Economist, EEF, the manufacturers' organization

There are a lot of ifs. If we have a referendum in the summer or Autumn of 2016, and if the polls are close, then it is pretty likely we'd see confidence among businesses to invest, in particular, take a pause in the run up to the vote. Around 40% of EEF's manufacturing members have told us that they see potential uncertainty around the UK's place in the EU as a business risk in 2016. But this is unlikely to be enough to put a material dent in growth in 2016—regardless of the outcome.

Longer term, the potential is for more negative consequences if Britain's votes to leave the EU, especially given the complexity of the divorce proceedings. We'd be looking at least two years of difficult negotiations, during which we'd expect a hiatus on investment activity.

Steve Hughes, Head of Economic and Social Policy, Policy Exchange

a.) Not much. The referendum is unlikely to be held until September at the earliest, so there will only be three months for it to make an impact. Any impact will depend on public confidence in the exit plans laid out in the campaign and its immediate aftermath by those that wish to leave.

b.) That all depends on what a post-Brexit relationship with the EU looks like, and how long it is expected to take to reach whatever that new relationship is. We are nowhere near knowing what the answers to either of these questions are—although the campaign will inevitably tease at least some of this out.

Ethan Ilzetzki, Lecturer in Economics, London School of Economics

The political classes seem to be taking a "remain" result for granted, despite polls running very close. A "leave" result would likely take a majority of observers by surprise. There is a substantial risk, therefore, that this result would rattle markets and create economic and policy uncertainty. The longer term implications would be negative, but it is very difficult to ascertain their magnitude. The devil will, as always, be in the details. Will the UK have a free-trade agreement with the EU after departure? Will the UK continue to accept EU migrants—who make a net positive contribution to this country—after leaving?

Richard Jeffrey, Chief Investment Officer, Cazenove Capital Management

In the short term, a vote to leave the EU would result in prolonged period of uncertainty, lasting around two years. Inevitably, there would be an impact on trade flows with the EU, although any damage to exports of goods and financial services would be partially offset by lower imports of consumer and capital goods. However, inwards investment would decline and it is also likely that domestic industry would put investment plans on hold for a period. This could have a more significant impact on growth during the transition period. I do not anticipate that there would be a significant impact on household or government spending. Once the exit terms had been negotiated (and I assume it would be in the interests of both parties to agree a "clean" exit), the UK could become a more attractive base for foreign companies looking for an European base. One specific area of the economy that could benefit would be financial services. Therefore, the medium term implications of Brexit could be modestly positive.

Oliver Jones, Economist, Fathom Consulting

A vote to leave the EU in 2016 could have a significant impact in terms of confidence and would lead us to revise down our forecasts. The biggest effect would be uncertainty—both in the run up to the referendum, and afterwards in the event of a vote to leave. It would take several years to be sure about the structure of Britain's relationship with the EU after a vote to leave: would we participate in an arrangement like Norway or Switzerland, or would some other arrangement be put in place. While those uncertainties remained unresolved, investment would be likely to be the hardest-hit area, undermining growth in both the short and the long term.

Dhaval Joshi, Chief strategist, BCA Research

Brexit would not directly change the prospects for 2016 because the referendum is likely to be at the back end of the year. Nevertheless, uncertainty about the vote outcome could weigh on the economy, as some long-term spending commitments were put on hold.

Brexit would be a negative shock to the economy in the medium term because foreigners would reassess the UK's merits as a destination for foreign direct investment. Also, while multinationals would certainly maintain a significant toehold in the UK, their centre of gravity would inevitably move closer to the core EU.

DeAnne Julius, former MPC member, now Chair of UCL
I would expect a month or two of financial market volatility to follow a Leave vote, and anxiety by certain business segments but not a significant hit to growth either in the short or medium term.

Stephen King, HSBC, Senior Economic Adviser
If by "next year" you're referring to 2016, the answer is "not much" —partly because the vote isn't likely to come through until later in the year.

If by "next year," you're referring to 2017, the answer is "possibly quite a lot." There would be huge political turmoil in Westminster —particularly with regard to finding a successor for Cameron— a very uncertain divorce negotiation with the European Union, growing pressure from Scotland for another referendum vote, a potentially massive legislative programme to create new UK laws to replace existing European laws and, at the very least, bemusement on behalf of countries outside Europe as to the UK's economic and political prospects. However, there would also possibly be big questions about the EU's future: populists in other European countries would doubtless regard the UK's exit as an opportunity to force through radical political reform.

The evidence is very mixed. It's worth noting that, of the bigger economies in Europe, the UK has consistently been one of the better performers as measured by GDP per capita since around 1980, only a handful of years after the UK first joined. It may be that, for all the criticism, the UK has actually flourished within the European Union. Footballers that leave clubs where they have done well have sometimes underperformed thereafter: just think of Fernando Torres at Liverpool and then at Chelsea. Could the UK be heading the same way?

Simon Kirby, Head of Macromodelling and Forecasting, NIESR
The 12 to 24 month period after such a vote would probably prove quite volatile for the UK economy. There will probably induce greater uncertainty around various negotiations with trading partners and with the EU in particular. I'm going to avoid the

medium to long-run prospects questions as I do not want to pre-empt the answers from research published in the coming months, including by some of my colleagues at NIESR.

James Knightley, Senior Economist, ING

Confidence would take a severe hit given business surveys show the majority of companies are pro-EU membership. It would therefore create significant uncertainty that will hurt business investment and hiring. Sterling would likely fall and the BoE could reverse course on any policy tightening. I would therefore see a significant hit to near-term activity, but assume a trade deal would get agreed fairly quickly and the more stimulative monetary conditions could actually see 2H17-2018 growth do better than would otherwise happen. Longer term implication depend on what the UK can achieve with its new found "freedoms," but it would also ensure another Scottish Independence referendum, that could drag the UK economy back into the mire.

Ashwin Kumar, Director, Liverpool Economics

The prospect of a referendum will increase economic uncertainty, reducing investment and growth below their potential.

Ruth Lea, Arbuthnot Banking Group, Economic Adviser

There would be very little difference for 2016. Trade with the EU & investment activity would continue much as usual even if a 2016 referendum supported Brexit.

Improve prospects: the UK would be able to appeal/amend irksome regulations (eg employment legislation, but not so much product regulations which tend to be agreed internationally), would be able to negotiate its own trade deals, would be able to run a non-discriminatory immigration policy without having to favour EU nationals and would no longer be a major net contributor the EU budget.

All these would help the UK's medium-term prospects.

Grant Lewis, Head of Research, Daiwa Capital Markets Europe

A vote to leave the EU will inevitably have an impact on the UK's growth prospects. In the short term the main effect is likely to come through weaker business confidence, and hence weaker investment. So growth in 2016 and into 2017 will be weaker than otherwise would have been the case. The longer-term impact will inevitably depend on the nature of the UK's eventual relationship with the EU. A settlement that resembles EU membership, albeit without any say in the rules, need not necessarily have too large an impact on long-term growth prospects, although certain sectors, such as finance, will likely suffer. Any settlement that sees UK access to EU markets restricted will clearly have a much greater impact on growth prospects—those who think that the Commonwealth can replace the EU as the UK's main trading partner are simply deluded about both the economics and the politics. And anything that stops or severely restricts the flow of migrants to the UK from the EU will have an inevitable impact on the country's potential growth rate.

John Llewellyn, Partner, Llewellyn Consulting

Prospects for next year would not change much, on the assumption that any vote comes late in the year, although pro-Brexit polls in the run-up could begin to dent investment.

But in 2017 and beyond, investment could fall off significantly. And there could well be retaliation in the UK's European export markets. This is a risk that the UK does not need.

Gerard Lyons, Chief Economic Adviser to Boris Johnson, the Mayor of London,

(a) The question assumes the outcome of a Referendum will be a Brexit. I would expect the Referendum debate to highlight the democratic deficit as the key issue, given the political focus of the EU project. But, in terms of economics, if the No campaign wins—as this question assumes—then it will have been able to paint a vision of how the UK will thrive and prosper outside of the EU. If that is the case then the impact of a Brexit on business and consumer confidence may be muted. Nonetheless, even though Brexit should not damage the UK in the medium term it is equivalent to an economic shock and thus would likely have a temporary near-term impact. Also, regarding the impact in 2016, another key issue is when a Referendum may take place. It could even be as early late June 2016, allowing for the four month campaign, and ahead of a likely escalation of the migrant crisis this summer. It should be said that remaining in the EU also contains considerable uncertainty—such as the future relationship between the euro zone and the non euro zone and consequences of ever closer union—yet in 2016 it is the uncertainty associated with a Brexit that will likely attract attention in terms of the economic impact. It is hard to quantify this, but one would expect there to be both uncertainty ahead of, and immediately after, a no vote. The market consensus was wrong ahead of Black Wednesday, when sterling left the ERM, expecting it to push rates higher and trigger a recession, it of course had the opposite impact. Leaving the EU is different to leaving the ERM, not least because of the need to negotiate an exit and future relationship, but the consensus may also be too pessimistic about the impact of Brexit, and the Referendum campaign should allow a clear positive future vision of Brexit to be outlined.

(b) The medium term outlook for the UK with Brexit is positive. One way to picture the economic impact of a Brexit may be the shape of a letter "V" or a "tick." That is, Brexit may be like an economic shock, leading to near-term uncertainty over the future relationship with the EU and as the UK has to establish a framework for trade deals. The reality is that the key issue is not only whether one is in or out of the EU but what one does inside, or outside. In the medium-term, Brexit would be better for the economy than remaining in an unreformed EU. The best scenario would be a truly reformed EU, but instead of the present debate being an opportunity for the EU to focus on how it reforms—boosting demand, reducing unemployment, having an affordable social welfare system, being outward looking and innovative—it has been characterised more as British problem. That suggests significant reform is unlikely. So the choice may be a stark one, between the UK being in an EU that is inward looking, insular as the EU's share of the world economy shrinks or outside, trading with the whole world including Europe, negotiating our own, better suited, trade deals with a focus on what the UK is good at. Trade deals that should be quicker to negotiate, bespoke, clearly understood, iterative and enforceable. Europe's economic model is backward looking, with high rates of unemployment, and is unfit to position Europe well in a changing global economy. That is why it must reform. The UK needs to pursue a global agenda—and the issue is whether it is able to do that in a reformed EU or whether it needs to pursue that approach outside.

George Magnus, Senior economic adviser, UBS

A mid year referendum that resulted in a Brexit decision would most probably have a significant impact on sterling fairly quickly, which would worsen the Bop position up front, and growth. Capex and employment growth expectations would be scaled back. We would end 2016 on a worse footing than we started, with negative consequences cumulating into 2017 and the medium-term. A cheaper pound though might help at the margin.

Chris Martin, Professor of Economics, University of Bath

a) not much; Brexit is not a short-term issue

b) very much; Brexit would be an economic disaster.

Michael McMahon, Associate Professor of Economics, University of Warwick

a) On the announcement of a vote resulting in Brexit, I expect there would be some financial volatility and potentially some corporates would scale back or even cease their investment plans as they wait to determine whether (and to what extent) the UK will remain a base for their operations or whether they would be better off operating within the EU borders.

b) I think there is a medium term reduction in UK prospects through the likely reduction in the UK's attractiveness as a base for operations in the European Union (discussed above). Additionally, I think that inward (and outward) migration currently has a positive effect on UK medium term growth prospects and Brexit would also reduce this. Perhaps I would say that as a EU migrant!

Costas Milas, Professor, University of Liverpool
A Brexit outcome will make me more pessimistic for our growth prospects in (the second half of) 2016 and the medium term. Those arguing for a British exit from the EU have failed to present an economically convincing argument of the Brexit advantages. So if the British electorate vote in favour of Brexit, we will witness huge investor uncertainty and as a result, a (much) higher rate of return investors demand to be compensated for the greater risk they are willing to take in order to hold UK debt. This higher yield will add to the cost of borrowing that companies face and will delay their investment decisions. Consequently, economic growth will take a big hit in the second half of the year and beyond.

Patrick Minford, Professor of applied economics, Cardiff Business School, Cardiff University
Not at all in the short term. Not much will happen as the negotiations run on for two years. I have always said it will be Breset not Brexit; ie the UK needs to get a new serious relationship with the rest of EU that allows proper UK self-government, especially in vital trade and regulative areas, and yet preserves the many useful areas of co-operation. I have little doubt also that the many vested interests that gain from EU protection will be awarded fairly long transitional arrangements under the negotiations.

In the medium and long term Breset will herald a major growth-boosting period as the UK breaks free of the over-mighty EU with its protectionist mindset and establishes free trade and intelligent regulation aimed at UK economic interests.

Allan Monks, JPM Research, Economist

A vote to leave would create significant political and economic uncertainty, with the UK's large current account deficit magnifying the potential impact of a drop in investor confidence. This could be damaging for near term growth and employment prospects, and would give the MPC another reason to delay policy tightening. If Scottish voters to remain within the EU, this would create stronger grounds for the SNP to call for another referendum on independence—although the sharp drop in the price of oil has certainly weakened the economic argument for independence. One of the biggest challenges in the negotiations will be brokering a free-trade agreement for the UK with the rest of the EU. The existing models used by Switzerland and Norway will look unattractive to the UK. The UK's bargaining position is weakened by the fact it sends a much greater proportion of exports to the EU (45%) than the rest of Europe exports to the UK (10%). Any new free trade arrangement for the UK would come with strings attached. One irony of Brexit is that it would most likely involve the UK signing up to many regulations and standards that were a key reason for the discontent with EU membership in the first place.

Kathrin Muehlbronner, Moody's, Senior Vice President—Sovereign Risk Group

A vote to leave would be negative for growth in our view, not only for 2016 but also for 2017. Investment in particular would likely be negatively affected, given the uncertainty over what arrangements would replace EU membership. We expect that the UK government would aim to find a new trade arrangement with the EU that replicates at least some of the benefits that EU membership affords. But this would take time to negotiate. Exports would also be affected if exit from the EU resulted in the imposition of tariffs and non-tariff barriers.

The medium-term outlook would depend to an important extent on the kind of new trade arrangement with the EU that the UK would achieve as well as other policy choices of the UK government with regards to trade, regulatory and immigration policies. A Swiss-style series of bilateral agreements or a more comprehensive free trade agreement would replicate many of the advantages of EU membership. Neither would be easy or quick to achieve, however, implying a potentially prolonged period of uncertainty, which in itself is damaging to confidence and investment. Exit would also increase domestic political risk and might reduce the predictability and effectiveness of economic policymaking. Another referendum on Scottish independence would become more likely. In addition, the UK government would need to renegotiate a whole series of trade agreements with other countries and regions, besides negotiating with the EU.

Erik Nielsen, Global Chief Economist, UniCredit
Brexit would inject huge uncertainty for the outlook. I assume that Cameron would step down, and one of the Eurosceptic (or anti-EU) Tories would become PM. And I assume that the noise about Scotland would re-emerge, possibly leaving to another referendum on independence—and maybe to a break-up of the UK. From here, the issue is whether the UK (or what's left of it) would follow Norway in taking everything from Brussels (unlikely), or try to negotiate everything (Switzerland model)—likely, but outcome very tough to assume would always be a positive one.

Charles Nolan, Professor, University of Glasgow
The short term outlook for investment would likely worsen somewhat as would, I fear, the medium term outlook.

David Owen, Chief European Economist, Jefferies
On balance, we expect the UK to vote in favour of remaining in the EU, but the uncertainty created by the vote and what exactly happens in the case of a disorderly exit could have a major effect on the pattern of spending particularly in the one or two quarters surrounding the decision. It could also push back the timing of the first rate rise in the UK well into 2016 and potentially 2017.

In the case of an exit we can expect the rating agencies to downgrade the UK and for investors to focus much more attention on the UK's large current account deficit. Reserve managers will ultimately probably end up holding fewer Gilts, pushing up long term interest rates and sterling would weaken. One or two quarters of negative GDP are certainly possible, with the BoE adding liquidity on demand and potentially relaxing policy. In an ideal world they would have already got the Bank Rate up to a level where rates could be cut significantly again, but that will not be the case by a mid-2016 vote. A further round of QE is certainly possible, but any sharp sell-off in the pound would obviously complicate the policy decision. However, in a macro sense a weaker pound is precisely what would probably be required to generate stronger growth and capital inflows again.

Economically and politically the UK would certainly be viewed as significantly weaker, especially if there were further calls to break-up the Union, with the SNP demanding another referendum on Scotland's future. The fallout for investment and foreign direct and portfolio investment flows would be significant, especially in a protracted period of negotiations with the eventual out-turn far from clear. However, the idea that the UK could break away from the rest of the EU and for there to be no wider consequences for Europe more generally is simply fanciful. On a 3 year view there would still be a cost for countries like Italy and Spain in terms of what they yielded over Germany. In the absence of more wide-ranging structural reforms, Europe is perceived as a low growth bloc anyway. And, without the UK's much faster trend rate of growth (and not just because of EU migration), the rest of the EU would have far less political clout in the world. Which is one reason why we think a compromise will be achieved.

Joseph Pearlman, Professor of Economics, City University

a) make me more pessimistic as there will be smaller numbers of skilled workers entering the UK job market, and the UK might face increased tariffs on exports to Europe.

b) unclear, since the government could react to short-term growth reductions by providing subsidies for in-house training, and might also generate more growth by providing more funds for government investment.

John Philpott, Director, The Jobs Economist

A Leave vote would not change my view about 2016, since most of the practical dislocation would be delayed for a while. I think exit would result in a modest reduction in medium term trend growth, due to a mix of lower inward investment, which would hit productivity, and the likelihood of tighter controls on immigration from EU member states.

Kallum Pickering, Senior UK Economist, Berenberg Bank

a) If the UK were to vote to leave, this would be the most significant downside risk to the economy in 2016. The risk of an immediate and strong weakening in economic activity would be very high. Consumer and business sentiment would decline sharply leading to a slowdown in consumption and business investment. The cause would be a sharp rise in uncertainty about how a Brexit would be managed—what would be the future of London and how would Britain's trade relationship with its biggest market the EU develop? These would be two of the most pressing issues.

b) Medium-term prospects for the economy would be markedly weaker and policy support would be required. Our expectation that the Bank of England would be able to execute a gradual hiking cycle beginning in 2016 would be at serious risk.

Christopher Pissarides, Regius Professor of Economics, London School of Economics

It will negatively change my views about next year because of the uncertainty about the mechanics of exit and the new arrangements with the EU. The impact of these uncertainties could be substantial. I would still be less optimistic about the medium term because I don't think Britain will get as good a deal out of the EU as it now has, or as good as Norway currently has.

Ian Plenderleith, former MPC member

(a) Material damage to confidence, with immediate braking effect on growth.

(b) Material deterioration.

Jonathan Portes, Principal Research Fellow, National Institute of Economic and Social Research

I'd divide this into three:

a) short-term: relatively little visible impact. No doubt there would be some turbulence in financial markets, but I doubt we'd see much impact on the real economy in the very short-term (ie next year).

b) medium-term (ie the period of the negotiation over terms of exit and post-exit relationship between the EU and the UK, lasting at least 2 years). Significantly negative. These negotiations would be protracted, complex and probably acrimonious, leading to considerable uncertainty for both UK companies trading with the EU and international investors (not to mention EU citizens resident in the UK and vice versa). All this would be likely to have a substantial and negative impact on business confidence, business investment, FDI, and possibly trade and migration.

c) longer-term (post the negotiations and any transition)—impossible to forecast with any precision at this point, given we have very little idea of what the outcome of the negotiations in b) would be. The UK could undoubtedly survive and prosper outside the EU, and in some respects (flexibility on some aspects of trade and migration policy and regulation, reduced contributions to the EU budget) might benefit; but there are obvious and serious risks, in particular to trade in services (including financial services) which are vital to the UK economy and will become even more so in the next few decades.

Adam Posen, President, Peterson Institute for International Economics

If the British electorate vote to leave the EU in 2016, it changes my views about 2016 and the medium term drastically for the worse.

Business investment will dry up rapidly, and greater uncertainty premia will get built into interest rates. Trade with Euro Area will start declining, and that decline will increase over time. Sterling might start to crash forcing a Bank of England tightening. Real estate market would likely have some air taken out of it. Huge self-inflicted wound.

Vicky Pryce, Chief Economic Adviser, CEBR

Prospects likely to worsen if a referendum is held in 2016 and the result is 'no' as the outlook for investment, including from abroad, will worsen while negotiations of the terms of a new relationship with Europe begin. The political fallout from it will inevitably impact negatively on growth for years after. If the referendum is postponed then uncertainty remains for longer and will weigh heavily on the markets through 2016. Only prospect of improvement on forecasts for 2016 would be a clear and overwhelming vote to stay in.

Victoria Redwood, Chief UK Economist, Capital Economics

A vote to leave the EU in 2016 would clearly increase the uncertainty the UK would face, as there could be up to two years of exit negotiations. In that case, the UK's economic performance would probably be a bit weaker than our current forecast.

However, our views about the medium term prospects would not change much. Just as the potential gains from leaving have probably been overestimated, so have the potential costs. We think that the UK will do well whether in or out of the EU.

Ricardo Reis, Professor of Economics, London School of Economics

It would greatly increase my uncertainty on the prospects, at all horizons. There is little guidance on what exact policies would be adopted after the vote and, while leaving the EU could allow for some policy improvements, it would also open way for a whole list of dreadful policies regarding trade, immigration, and industrial policy that membership in the EU now precludes. Overall, my growth forecasts would probably go down, but much more important, my uncertainty about these forecasts would increase very much.

David Riley, BlueBay Asset Management, Head of Credit Strategy

The uncertainty generated by a pending and closely contested EU exit referendum could discourage consumption and investment spending and result in weaker growth in 2016 than currently forecast. A vote in favour of exit from the EU would render the medium-term outlook highly uncertain and generate volatility in financial markets until businesses and investors have clarity on the terms of the UK's exit and its ongoing commercial relationship with the EU.

Bridget Rosewell, Senior Adviser, Volterra Partners

I don't think that Brexit makes any real underlying difference, and indeed the advantages and disadvantages of membership of the EU (as distinct from a common trade area) are finely balanced.

However, uncertainty and political disruption could make a difference and will certainly affect Scotland and Northern Ireland.

Philip Rush, Nomura, Senior European Economist

There is a bifurcation in the growth outlook beyond the referendum. A vote to leave would introduce uncertainty, discouraging investment and potentially challenging the current account's financing to the point that the currency falls, importing inflation and hitting real incomes and growth. This would lower our growth forecast immediately following an out vote. However, as we expect the referendum in September 2016, most of the pain would be felt in 2017.

After the risk premium driven shock, there will be transitional costs into whatever the UK's new relationship is and these costs will be front-loaded. The negotiation of the UK's relationship with the remaining EU could take up to two years, so for most normal forecasting horizons, there will be downside news from a vote for Brexit. However, it is possible that the UK negotiates a better position outside the EU that allows a brisker pace of growth to be achieved beyond that. It may take a long time before the front loaded costs are recovered, if they ever are.

Michael Saunders, Citi

Pre-referendum uncertainty may cap business investment in 2016, but the adverse effect on the economy of a vote for Brexit in 2016 would be mainly felt in later years.

The UK economy at present is one of the major winners from globalisation, combining relatively low levels of regulation in the labour and product markets with (as an EU member) a high degree of open trade access globally. The UK stands out among major advanced economies in being able to achieve high inflows of foreign investment, a very high employment rate with high pay levels. Brexit would put that at risk, and would represent a retreat from globalisation, making the UK a less attractive place for business location. This is the biggest threat to the UK economic outlook and one of the top global uncertainties for 2016.

Andrew Sentance, Former MPC member and senior economic adviser, PwC

It would not change my view of economic prospects for next year very much but would make me more negative about the medium-term, for 2 reasons. (1) Disruption and uncertainty created by Brexit; (2) Lack of a clear alternative to underpin UK's trade and investment relationships, which have supported UK growth while we have been EU members. It is worth noting that once the UK escaped from the 1970s doldrums, it has achieved the strongest growth of GDP/head of any G7 economy from 1980. This period contrasts with the 1950s and 1960s before the UK joined the EEC/EU when our economy was in serious relative decline.

However, I have more confidence in the British electorate. I predict we will vote to stay in the EU.

Philip Shaw, Chief Economist, Investec

a) On the basis of a mid-2016 "leave" vote, it is difficult to see a sudden and abrupt slowdown in spending and so activity should have enough momentum to carry it through the rest of the year.

b) Medium-term prospects are a different matter entirely. Inward investment would probably dry up, while uncertainty over EU trade access might well slow domestic capital spending and, of course, exports. But there are implications for Britain's internal dynamics, as well as its relationship with the rest of Europe. A 'leave' vote risks prompting Scotland to push for another referendum on independence, which if granted, could put a possible break-up of the UK back on to the agenda.

Andrew Simms, Director, New Weather Economics

Uncertainty and instability are the enemies of real prosperity. Solutions to pressing problems that range from migration to climate change and financial crime require international collective action, which a British exit from the EU would seriously undermine. The uncertainty it would create would be widely destabilising and worsen the prospects for progress in any of these areas. Simultaneously it is likely to complicate economic life in Europe still further and make solving existing problems to do with the European Union harder.

In the medium term, I suspect that Brexit would expose as illusory its advocates' stated aims of greater policy sovereignty, simplicity and freedom from reciprocal obligations and social and environmental responsibility. The sheer complexity of continuing European and global economic interdependence would replace one Europe-wide set of agreements with a thicket of even more. In this circumstance, all sorts of prospects would become trickier and harder still to navigate.

Andrew Smith, Chief Economic Adviser, Industry Forum

(a) Although a vote to leave would increase uncertainty, coming next summer at the earliest I doubt it would have much impact on the economic outcome for the year as a whole.

(b) Further out, though—for several years at least—I would expect the effect to be unambiguously negative. We cannot count on the EU being prepared to grant continued access to the European market on the same privileged terms, particularly if the divorce turns vitriolic (contrary to received wisdom, in terms of trade flows "they" do not need "us" as much as we need them). And, if it were so easy to expand trade with the rest of the world to compensate, you would expect that to be happening already."

Don Smith, Deputy Chief Investment Officer, Brown Shipley

Whatever the view on whether the UK would be better or worse-off outside the EU over the longer term, the uncertainty generated by a decision to leave the EU would undoubtedly be damaging for sterling assets across the board and, indeed, the value of sterling on foreign exchanges. Consumer confidence would be lower, business confidence and investment intentions would also very likely be negatively impacted. The fallout would take time to fully materialise although growth would probably be a little weaker during 2016 in this event.

Andrew Smithers, Retired

I hope we don't leave the EU but for political rather than economic reasons. Leaving is likely to make little difference either next year or in the medium term, unless if helps by pushing down sterling.

Peter Spencer, Professor of Economics, University of York

a) I doubt that a vote to leave would have much impact on activity in 2016 year, though uncertainty in the run up to the poll and subsequent negotiations over the UK's access to the single market could be very damaging for investment in the second half.

b) Longer term, everything would hang on how those negotiations went, but I doubt they would go well. It is all very well to say that we import more from Europe than we export—but what does that say about the state of British manufacturing industry? Could we really pretend that we could do without those imports? Would UK consumers really be prepared to drive around in British

Leyland cars (assuming that outfit or its like could somehow be resurrected) rather than BMWs? What sort of bargaining point is that?

James Sproule, Chief Economist, IoD

My expectation is for the UK to vote to stay, but narrowly, and for the Brexit question to remain pertinent. If we were to vote to leave, the degree of uncertainty is likely to cause a drying up of investment both in the UK and the wider EU.

Ian Stewart, Chief Economist, Deloitte

Exiting the EU opens up the possibility of profound change in the UK's legal, regulatory, trading and fiscal arrangements. The period of uncertainty that would follow and exit vote would dampen business sentiment and soften growth prospects in the near term. But with inflation subdued the Bank of England would be well placed to try to counter such effects by running easier monetary policy. Much of the activity that vanished in the wake of Brexit would be displaced rather than destroyed, and growth rates would move back to around trend rates on a 3-5 year view.

Gary Styles, Director, GPS Economics

a.) The short run impact would be very small (concealed in the rounding).

b.) The medium term outlook is a much tougher ask under this scenario. Higher levels of policy and economic uncertainty will drive economic growth lower. Interest rates are likely to move higher and inward investment lower.

Phil Thornton, Lead consultant, Clarity Economics

The uncertainty over the timing and outcome of a referendum in 2016 has probably been priced in by the markets and by businesses so perhaps no immediate impact. The medium-term outlook depends on any forecaster's views of the pros and cons of leaving. My opinion is that the decision to leave will create more uncertainty that will continue as negotiations for a post-EU world rumble on, the City of London will suffer, and foreign investors may well think twice about current or future investments this side of the Channel. So negative.

David Tinsley, UK and European economist, UBS

The uncertainty generated by the EU referendum vote in the run up clearly has the capacity to restrain business investment growth next year. Moreover, should the vote result in the UK leaving the EU there will be a protracted period of uncertainty over the UK's position vis-à-vis the EU for some time to come. That again could put a break on growth, and indeed potentially delay the Bank of England tightening cycle by some way.

The medium term consequences of BREXIT would depend critically on what type of trading relationships with the remaining EU were negotiated. Under the assumption that a relatively liberal trading arrangement was agreed, the medium-term consequences for the UK's long-run growth rate would probably not be very high, although the economy could still suffer a once-off fall in the level of output.

Samuel Tombs, Pantheon Macroeconomics, Chief UK economist

A Brexit would subdue investment and exports immediately, even if it took time for the terms of the UK's exit to be negotiated. Borrowing costs would rise and sterling would be vulnerable to falling sharply, boosting inflation, if overseas investors became hesitant about lending to the UK.

The potential economic benefits of leaving the EU—greater freedom to negotiate trade agreements and decreased regulation, particularly for the City—will take several years to be felt. A convincing case has not been made yet that these long-run benefits justify the near-term disruption and the loss of unfettered access to the single market.

Kitty Ussher, Managing Director, Tooley Street Research

(a) a vote to leave in 2016 would have a very negative short- to medium-term effect on the investment climate mainly through the uncertainty that it would create as to what precisely will change and when.

(b) In the in the medium to long term, the trend rate of GDP growth will be a little lower due to reduced competitive pressure on UK firms from possible implied or real trade barriers and the negative signal sent to prospective investors seeking to trade with the EU from Britain.

John van Reenen, Director, Centre for Economic Performance

The direct effects on incomes and GDP would be long-term and obviously depend on the exact negotiations of what follows. Under a pessimistic scenario we have estimated losses of real income over the long-run of 6-9% of real incomes.

There are losses of 2% even under a more optimistic situation where we are in EEA like Norway. In addition to a loss of trade there will be a loss of foreign investment and less inward migration from highly talented Europeans who have aided UK growth. The idea that we'll be able to strike lots of new free trade deals with other countries being free from EU is fantasy, as is the idea that there will be some bonfire of red tape that lights up UK growth. Scotland will be lost and we will have an ongoing degree of uncertainty that will depress us economically, politically and culturally for many years to come.

Daniel Vernazza, Lead UK Economist, UniCredit

In the event of Brexit, the economic uncertainty (it will take up to two years to negotiate the terms of exit) and political uncertainty (Cameron would surely have to stand down) will significantly weigh on economic activity.

In the medium term, it seems likely that the UK's relationship with the EU will not be that different from the current arrangement —it simply has too much to lose otherwise. Ironically, the UK will likely end up with less say, unilaterally adopting most EU legislation. So, while the medium- to long-term impact of leaving the EU will be negative, it will probably be modestly so.

Sushil Wadhwani

I believe that the fear of Brexit is already having an adverse impact on economic activity, in that it is leading to a postponement of decisions relating to FDI and corporate investment more generally.

If we did vote to leave, I think that, in the first instance, the size of these effects would be amplified, and consumer confidence would probably also suffer at that point. This would weaken the economy considerably during the fourth quarter of 2016.

The impact on medium-term prospects is more difficult to predict as it does depend on the precise post-exit arrangements with the European Union, as this will determine the degree to which we lose the benefits of belonging to a large, relatively integrated market.

Peter Warburton, Chief Economist, Economic Perspectives

a) Brexit would be more likely to hurt imports than exports. Expect to see a weakening of Sterling in the lead up to the referendum, and probably to remain weaker afterwards.

b) Brexit is likely to have little impact in the medium term on UK growth. There is a chance that it will lead to higher inflation. The money that is currently being used to pay the UKs EU contribution could potentially be diverted into funding a tax cut to improve competitiveness, potentially cutting corporation tax, for example.

Simon Wells, HSBC, Chief UK Economist

If Britain votes to leave the EU in 2016, the near-term impact would be hugely increased economic uncertainty. In the near term, there may no clarity about the post-EU arrangements. The economic implications of a "soft exit" (eg remaining in the EEA) could be very different to a "hard exit" (eg being no more part of the EU than the US is). The uncertainty during the period of divorce negotiation could lead to investment decisions being delayed. This mammoth task would also divert government and civil service resources away from other areas of policymaking.

There is no evidence that being a member of the EU has harmed the UK economy and it may well have benefited. Pragmatically, it is hard to see a post-EU deal that would place huge restrictions on UK-EU goods trade, which would be mutually destructive. The uncertainty lies in potential barriers to services trade, which is important to the UK given its expertise and trade surplus in services with the EU. But the longer-term assessment of the impact of EU withdrawal will have to be made over several decades.

Mike Wickens, Professor of Economics, Cardiff University and University of York

a) In the short term Brexit would probably be a negative shock to the economy due to greater uncertainty about the future.

b) In the longer term the economy should benefit from becoming more efficient, competitive and open. The main danger to this is that the EU. to its own detriment, tries to erect tariff barriers to the UK.

Neil Williams, Group Chief Economist, Hermes Investment Management

The big known unknown for 2016! Logic suggests the UK not wanting to distance itself from its main trading partner, risking FDI, and diluting its political relationship with the US.

But, leaving would raise recession risk, take the shine off the pound, and question who's going to buy the gilts—given around one-third of our £1.3tr conventional gilts is held by international investors who'll care about currency and credit-ratings. Domestically-led Japan got away without a buyers strike, but if we can't, would the BoE have to reactivate QE?

Chris Williamson, Chief Economist, Markit

Growth next would be lower due to the uncertainty and disruptions caused by Brexit, especially in relation to trade. It could easily knock 0.5% off growth while also deterring investment and hiring to a significant extent.

Longer term, I'd expect a net negative impact to persist, based on research which shows most major companies perceive EU membership to be beneficial.

Richard Woolhouse, Chief Economist, BBA

a) Clearly it would increase uncertainty as the terms of UK engagement with the EU would need to be "renegotiated." This is very unlikely to be a costless exercise.

b) UK is a significant recipient of FDI and many invest in the UK for access to the EU market.

In addition, exit would likely be a negative for parts of the City—in particular, the global investment banks.

Many US investment banks organise their EU and Emea operations from London and would need to be confident of retaining the benefits of the passporting regime.

The UK has also gained significantly in terms of its share of Euro denominated activity in the last 15 years and many European banks have located their wholesale banking activities in the UK as a result—this trend would very likely be reversed should a Brexit occur.

Tony Yates, Professor of Economics, University of Birmingham; Centre for Macroeconomics at the LSE

My best guess would be that not much would happen in the short term, but in the longer term the trajectory for potential output would be somewhat weaker. That said, there are big risks, and they are all to the downside. The referendum itself may provoke market panic, and there will be several key event risks after that, all of which could trigger market runs, if for no reason than people think they will. Location decisions feature strategic complementarities strongly. [Whether it's good for me to be here depends on whether you will be here]. Circumstances like this can mean large and sudden changes in location—read direct investment and other capital flows—that could be highly damaging to a UK that looks like it might exit, or does.

Azad Zangana, Schroders, Senior European Economist & Strategist

It largely depends on when the referendum will be held. I think it will take place in the autumn, which leaves little time for an exit vote to have an impact on the economy in 2016. There could be a slowdown in business investment in the run up to and just after the referendum.

The final impact will be determined by the terms of exit, which could take two years to be negotiated. During this period, business investment, especially that funded by foreign direct investment flows could be adversely impacted.

Viewpoint 2

Will the EU Be OK?

Judy Dempsey

In the following viewpoint, Carnegie Europe nonresident senior fellow Judy Dempsey puts experts on the hot seat, asking them to consider whether the EU can carry on—bruised, improved, or not at all—without the UK. Varying notions are offered as to whether the EU will grow more fractured and short-sighted or seize this moment as an opportunity to strengthen alliances and its core mission.

A selection of experts answer a new question from Judy Dempsey on the foreign and security policy challenges shaping Europe's role in the world.

Rosa Balfour, Senior fellow in the Europe Program at the German Marshall Fund of the United States

Of course the EU can survive without Britain; the question is what kind of Europe it will be. Will it find the drive to reinvent itself for the twenty-first century, capable of addressing citizens' concerns about the future and helping shape a changing world? Or will it wither into an inward-looking rump EU focused on defending past glories and pursuing half-baked initiatives for short-term gains, doomed to decline? This is what is at stake.

The British departure accelerates the EU's need to reinvent itself but is not its cause. Believing that removing the British obstacle will set European integration in motion is fallacious. Brexit can be a transformational moment only if the EU seizes the opportunity

---

"Judy Asks: Can the EU Survive Without Britain?" by Judy Dempsey, Carnegie Europe, September 7, 2016. Reprinted by Permission.

to understand the causes of today's crises, rather than focus on the symptoms, and rethink the terms of integration.

Current European leaders seem to be dodging these issues. All the signs in the run-up to the first brainstorm among the 27 remaining member states in Bratislava on September 16 to discuss the future of Europe without the UK suggest that more muddling through will be on the menu for the year to come. European elites do not have the mandate from citizens to rejuvenate the EU; the upcoming electoral cycle is unlikely to allow for any bold initiative; and the sentiments that led a majority of British people to vote to leave the EU are shared by many across the Channel, making any path toward reinventing the EU mired by pitfalls.

Kris Bledowski, Council Director and Senior Economist at the Manufacturers Alliance for Productivity and Innovation

Yes, the EU can live on without the UK. After all, the union had functioned prior to 1973 as a small group without supposedly important members such as Poland, Spain, Sweden, or the UK. Over time, Britain became an influential component of the union but not an indispensable one, such as Germany.

The future heft of the European Union—with or without the UK—will hinge on its members agreeing to more than their narrow economic interests. The prominence of the UK in the EU lies in infusing Europe's policies with strategic thinking. On relations with Africa, India, Russia, or the United States, Britain sees far and wide. With its notable military weight and a history of deploying force, the UK brings a muscular complement to the EU's traditional soft power.

Britain also contributes comparative advantages to the EU through the country's financial services, diplomatic corps, and excellence in higher education. Members in the East and North of the union look up to the UK for help in building consensus when the going gets tough in ministerial deliberations. The European Union won't collapse after Brexit, but it will lose an influential voice.

Fraser Cameron, Director of the EU-Russia Center

Of course the EU can survive without Britain, but the question is: What kind of EU will it be? Losing the world's fifth-largest economy and the EU's strongest military power is a severe blow. The EU could possibly recover if it had more of a sense of purpose.

But the sense of drift in the EU has been apparent for many years, accentuated by a lack of vision, solidarity, and leadership. There is no consensus among the large member states on basic questions, but above all on economic policy. Far from cementing the union, the eurozone has contributed to its fracturing, while the refugee crisis has displayed an alarming deficit in solidarity. The design flaws in the euro were replicated in the Schengen passport-free zone, which without properly controlled external borders was destined to fail.

Even though not in the eurozone or Schengen, the UK was often used as a scapegoat, while others conveniently hid behind the all too frequent British veto. Without Britain, the EU has the chance to redefine itself and move forward. But discussions in advance of the September 16 summit in Bratislava of the remaining 27 member states show just how divided the EU is on most big issues.

The EU will no doubt survive. But unless it can restore economic growth, tackle the scourge of youth unemployment, and make itself more relevant to its citizens, there may be more exits around the corner.

István Hegedűs, Chairman of the Hungarian Europe Society

Yes, the EU can survive without Britain.

I disagree with arguments that it will be easier to reform the EU without the awkward Brits. Symbolically, the historic European project has suffered an unprecedented blow from the British vote to leave the union. Now, it will be much more difficult to energize the European elites to push the reset button for deeper political integration and a more supranational decisionmaking setup. Still, as a surprising number of demonstrations have shown in the UK since the shocking result of the June 23 referendum, pro-EU parties and politicians are not so lonely in their often uncertain efforts to keep the European construction working.

The multiple challenges facing the EU have strengthened populist forces all over the continent; many present not a cure but a clear danger to the European liberal democratic order. Some future political scenarios at the European and national levels may look shocking. Still, if democrats are able to change the general framing of public discourse from the politics of fear to the politics of vision, including a new narrative of a reinvented Europe, they might win in the long run. They have to find an emotional tone to supplement the rational arguments in favor of the EU cause.

Yet, politics is not just about smart communication techniques and a renewed language. The EU also needs self-confident democratic politicians in each member state.

Josef Janning, Head of the Berlin Office and Senior Policy Fellow at the European Council on Foreign Relations

Yes, the EU can survive, because it must—and it will do so for its own reasons. The June 23 popular vote in the UK to exit the European Union does not contradict the logic of integration, which is to sustain or regain the ability to shape Europe's destiny by pooling sovereignty. Europeans fare better together, to use the British government's slogan in the 2014 Scottish independence referendum campaign. It just so happens that a majority of British voters begged to differ when it came to EU membership. None of the goals of deeper integration—be it the single market, the Schengen passport-free zone, the common currency, or even the prospect of a common defense—has lost its plausibility because of Britain's refusal to participate.

However, some of the thinking traditionally associated with the EU will wither away. With the UK leaving, integration has become a two-way street; member states can travel in both directions. Britain's move may indeed tempt others and inspire more à la carte thinking, so there's a need to consider issues that countries can opt into as well as out of. Also, the notion of states maturing over the time of their engagement in the EU seems overly ambitious. Europe's nation-states have been around too long to adapt easily; integration should therefore build on strengthening the cooperative layers between governments rather than relying on the transformative power of supranational institutions.

Stefan Lehne, Visiting Scholar at Carnegie Europe

Certainly! Losing the UK is a sad outcome, but not a mortal blow, which the dropping out of Germany or France would be. In view of its opt-outs from the eurozone and the Schengen passport-free area, the UK has for a long time been a semidetached member state. Its departure weakens the EU but does not put its existence into question. In fact, polls across the continent following Britain's June 23 referendum decision to leave indicated an increase in support for the EU.

Sudden disintegration of the EU is therefore not a serious threat. The real risk is that the ongoing erosion of the cohesion and trust among member states will continue. In this case, the eurozone and Schengen would not be consolidated, important projects such as the energy union or a stronger EU foreign policy would remain stuck, and compliance with EU legislation would decay. This ever-looser union would formally still exist, but the real action would return to the (bigger) nation-states and to outside actors.

Reversing these trends is the main challenge of the September 16 summit of the 27 post-Brexit member states in Bratislava. This means rapidly pushing ahead with concrete action in priority areas like migration and security. But it also means gradually building consensus on a number of reform steps that could in the longer term deliver a more united and robust EU.

Bruno Maçães, Nonresident Associate at Carnegie Europe

No doubt. The EU is a multidimensional concept. In some of these dimensions, nothing of great significance will change. The euro area faces continuing challenges, but they have nothing to do with the United Kingdom. The EU as a regulatory power will very likely survive Britain's exit unaffected. The single market will project its influence over the UK as it does on a global scale.

The dimensions in which Brexit will be more deeply felt are foreign policy and security. The UK is a significant actor in these areas, and what is more, Brexit will leave the EU with reduced influence, prestige, and soft power. The image of disintegration in these areas is almost as negative as the reality. Therefore, whether the EU can survive as a major foreign policy actor without the UK is open to debate. My cautious answer is that it will struggle to do so.

John Peet, Political (and Brexit) Editor at the Economist

Yes, though it could be weaker and more fragmented. Britain has always been semidetached, refusing to join the club at first and then standing aside from the euro area, the Schengen passport-free zone, and large chunks of justice and home affairs cooperation. For this reason, Britain's exit will do less damage to the EU than the departure of any other large country would.

Yet the EU will suffer from losing a big member that has long had the strongest liberal, free-trading instincts. EU countries not in the eurozone will feel more anxious as the single currency area pursues deeper integration; the arrival of a multitier Europe of concentric circles will become more obvious. If Britain prospers post-Brexit, that will also encourage Euroskeptic forces in many other countries.

So although Brexit is likely to change the EU profoundly, it is unlikely to destroy it.

Marc Pierini, Visiting Scholar at Carnegie Europe

Yes, it can and it will. But how well the EU survives depends on how the 27 governments of the smaller European Union will organize themselves.

Undoubtedly, there are negative sides to Britain's decision to exit the EU. In economic terms, the EU is losing one of the three largest member countries. It is also losing a major diplomatic player and one of only two states (with France) with a sizable military projection capability.

Yet the positive aspects of Brexit are many, at least on paper. First is the psychological factor. With Britain out, the element of suspicion will also go out of the door. The lingering feeling that British exceptionalism was always an impediment to truly European policies should disappear, removing an obstacle to bolder decisions by some of the EU 27.

Second, despite the massive technical and political difficulties ahead, a clear and effective relationship can be built in a reasonable timeframe between Britain and the EU of 27 members.

A third aspect is that the future UK-EU framework might constitute a formula to accommodate Turkey's European ambitions, which cannot be fulfilled by accession.

Finally, Brexit gives an opportunity for some of the 27 members of the new EU to reorganize their relations in a stronger, more cohesive fashion. This may not necessarily involve all the remaining 27 governments and may lead to a core EU that subscribes to more ambitious goals than the rest of the bloc.

Eugeniusz Smolar, Senior Fellow at the Center for International Relations in Warsaw

Of course the EU can survive—and it (probably) will. There can be no time-out for deeper reflection, as a prolonged period of uncertainty would only deepen insecurity.

The EU's inner core will keep concentrating on solving the problems of the eurozone to create jobs around Europe. In the past, there was a lot of wheeling and dealing to keep the Brits, the Poles, the Swedes, and those in a few other non-eurozone states happy as they worried that decisions by members of the single currency might worsen their positions in the EU. With Britain's vote to exit the EU, there will be less hesitation to do what is necessary without paying too much attention to the rest of the crowd.

The EU must do much more to reassure concerned Europeans about security, as uncontrolled migration might lead

Notes on Brexit and the Pound

The much-hyped severe Brexit recession does not, so far, seem to be materializing—which really shouldn't be that much of a surprise, because as I warned, the actual economic case for such a recession was surprisingly weak. [...] But we are seeing a large drop in the pound, which has steepened as it becomes likely that this will indeed be a very hard Brexit. How should we think about this?

Originally, stories about a pound plunge were tied to that recession prediction: domestic investment demand would collapse, leading to sustained very low interest rates, hence capital flight. But the demand collapse doesn't seem to be happening. So what is the story?

For now, at least, I'm coming at it from the trade side—especially trade in financial services. It seems to me that one way to think about this is in terms of the "home market effect," an old story in trade but one that only got formalized in 1980.

Here's an informal version: imagine a good or service subject to large economies of scale in production, sufficient that if it's consumed in two countries, you want to produce it in only one, and export to the other, even if there are costs of shipping it. Where will this production be located? Other things equal, you would choose the larger market, so as to minimize total shipping costs. Other things may not, of course, be equal, but this market-size effect will always be a factor, depending on how high those shipping costs are.

In one of the models I laid out in that old paper, the way this worked out was not that all production left the smaller economy, but rather that the smaller economy paid lower wages and therefore made up in competitiveness what it lacked in market access. In effect, it used a weaker currency to make up for its smaller market.

— **"Notes on Brexit and the Pound," by Paul Krugman, The New York Times Company, October 11, 2016**

to the disintegration of the EU. The EU should also backtrack institutionally here and there—if only to signal to worried electorates that the whole process is under the control of national governments and parliaments. The time has come for good old politics at the expense of the much criticized but on the whole successful technocratic approach of yesteryear. The European Commission, whether that of President Jean-Claude Juncker or any other commission, will not be the source of solutions.

The most important priorities remain the EU's internal cohesion and a sense of purpose from the pro-European elites to translate the European project into language with which the people can associate.

Viewpoint 3

Fact-Checking the Brexit Campaigns

Ashley Kirk

In the following viewpoint, Ashley Kirk, a data journalist at the Telegraph, *fact-checks some of the many dubitable claims made on either side of the Brexit debate, noting that many of these claims directly resulted in the UK's decision on Brexit. Her work, done with Full Fact, one of the UK's foremost independent fact-checking organizations, provides insight into the opacity of the various campaigns, as many assertions prove difficult to pin down.*

The UK opted to leave the EU on 23 June 2016 after a campaign mired by scaremongering and the misuse of statistics.

Polls suggested a close race to the end, and Brexit ended up clinching victory with 51.9 per cent of the vote.

With conflicting facts thrown around by all sides in the campaign, The Telegraph teamed up with Full Fact to analyse and check the big claims of the campaign.

From the number of times the UK is outvoted on the continent, to the truth about our financial contribution to the EU, we aimed to debunk false claims and back up the truth.

This is now particularly important: some of these claims have helped swing the UK to Brexit, and now the country must face the consequences.

On the Amount of Money the UK Gives to the EU

Verdict: Wrong

EU membership does come at a financial cost. The UK pays more into the EU budget than it gets back. But it's not £350 million a week.

The UK's discount, or rebate, reduces what we would otherwise be liable to pay.

In 2015, we paid the EU an estimated £13 billion, or £250 million a week.

Some of that money came back in EU payments funnelled through the government, so the government's 'net contribution' was around £8.5 billion, or £160 million a week. The EU also spends money directly—in grants to British researchers, for instance.

On the UK's Economy and the EU

Verdict: Hard to Say

Most economists seem to agree that leaving the EU will cost the UK economically.

But the £4,300 figure is an unhelpful summary of the research done by the Treasury's economists. It supposes that we end up with an EU agreement like Canada, which allows for fairly free trade in goods but less free trade in services.

£4,300 should not be taken or presented as a prediction of the cost to families. There's too much uncertainty in the figures and the analysis is about how the overall size of the economy could be affected, not about households' incomes.

But even without the numbers, you can choose to trust the driving idea behind this research: fewer barriers to trade makes for stronger economies. In the same way, we can choose to trust a doctor telling us not to eat junk food without demanding they predict exactly what our weight will be next year.

On Brexit's Impact on the NHS

Verdict: Hard to Say

There are two parts to this claim, made by the leader of the Trades Union Congress (TUC). The figures add up and the claim has been properly qualified, but whether the gloomy NHS-related predictions are realised depends on future political decisions about how the budget is divided.

Most economists agree that the economy would suffer if we leave the EU, and O'Grady is using estimates made by the Institute for Fiscal Studies, an independent think-tank.

And for her NHS claim, she is simply comparing the budget for NHS England with the IFS estimates. £30bn is roughly a quarter of the NHS England budget, so enough to fund it for three months.

However, according to George Osborne and Alistair Darling's "Brexit-budget," future politicians will try and limit the impact on the NHS by raising taxes and cutting in other areas. They say the impact on the NHS could be as much projected to be £2.5bn—two per cent of the total budget.

On EU Red Tape in the UK

Verdict: Hard to Say

This claim is taken from a paper by the think tank Open Europe, which is flawed in a number of respects.

This figure is simply a total of projected costs, which the paper argues makes an annual amount of £33.4bn.

But some regulations produce benefits as well, which Open Europe estimates total £58.3bn. The claim ignores this figure on the basis that it may not have actually materialised. Of course, this applies to costs as well.

Open Europe itself notes that the projected benefits for the "top five costliest EU-derived regulations" outweighed the costs.

On the UK's Sovereignty in the EU

Verdict: Wrong

According to Sara Hagemann of UK in a Changing Europe: It is incorrect to say that the UK consistently loses in the EU.

Since 1999, when decision records became available from the EU Council where governments meet to negotiate and adopt policies, the UK has been in the minority (voting "No") on 57 legislative acts.

It has supported—and hence been in the majority—on 2,474 acts, and abstained on 70 occasions.

It is true that the UK votes against the majority more frequently than other member states, in particular during the last few years of David Cameron's Government. But the UK is not consistently outvoted in the EU.

On British Jobs and Their Reliance on the EU

Verdict: Wrong

This is wrong. The calculations behind the claim are flawed and the estimates on which it's based are old and have since been substantially revised.

Roughly 15 per cent of manufacturing jobs were directly linked to demand from other EU countries in 2014, according to figures from the Centre for Economics and Business Research.

That doesn't mean these jobs are dependent on the UK being an EU member. The link is with trade, which may or may not be affected depending on what deal a post-Brexit UK gets, led by a new Prime Minister.

And if exports elsewhere grew, even a decline in trade with the EU will not necessarily mean that jobs will be lost.

On Britain's Immigration Levels and the EU

Verdict: Hard to Say

The UK population—currently at 65 million—is expected to reach 70 million in 2027 and 75 million in 2042. They're uncertain estimates, not least because they involve tentative predictions on future immigration levels.

The Office for National Statistics is assuming a fall in net migration, from 300,000 a year to under 200,000 from 2020.

Under its variant scenarios, "low migration" of 100,000 would mean we'd hit 70 million in 2031, four years later than the main projection. The population wouldn't reach 70 million before 2040 if we had no net migration at all for the next two decades.

There's no single piece of research that fully answers questions about quality of life and social cohesion. However, experts at the Migration Observatory have produced overviews on immigrants' effect on public finances, public services, and 'social cohesion'.

On Brexit's Impact on the Pound and European Holidays

Verdict: Hard to Say

This claim is speculation, but the thinking behind it is reasonable. All the government is really saying is that the pound will lose its value in the immediate aftermath of Brexit. This has support from plenty of other sources and has been immediately proved right.

The Governor of the Bank of England said before the vote that "the recent behaviour of the foreign exchange markets suggest that were the UK to vote to leave the EU, sterling's exchange rate would fall further." The Bank didn't put a number on it, but other claims estimated falls from 10 per cent to 25 per cent by 2020.

Cameron drew on Treasury analysis suggesting that sterling would fall at least 12 per cent, and applies that to the average spend for an EU holiday. If you get fewer euros for your pound, a holiday in the Eurozone will cost more.

This sterling effect is an expected short-term consequence of a leave vote, but NIESR believes it would have a permanent impact.

If sterling recovered for some other reason, the impact on holiday prices would be reversed. And while the general train of thought is heading in the right direction, the exact destination—the £230 figure—is impossibly precise.

Viewpoint 4

Old England, New System

George Monboit

"Culture is not working." That's the rather provocative view Guardian *columnist and author George Monboit takes in the following viewpoint. Despite his concession that Brexit was empowered by a "gruesome collection of schemers, misfits, liars, [and] extremists," Monboit argues that the pro-Brexit vote was "the eruption of an internal wound, inflicted over many years by an economic oligarchy on the poor and the forgotten." The work now, Monboit says, is to build a new political and economic system that works for all Britons, minimizes insecurity, and restrains corporate power. Monboit is the author of* Captive State: The Corporate Takeover of Britain.

Let's sack the electorate and appoint a new one: this is the demand made by MPs, lawyers and the four million people who have signed the petition calling for a second referendum. It's a cry of pain, and therefore understandable, but it's also bad politics and bad democracy. Reduced to its essence, it amounts to graduates telling non-graduates "we reject your democratic choice."

Were this vote to be annulled (it won't be), the result would be a full-scale class and culture war, riots and perhaps worse, pitching middle class progressives against those on whose behalf they've claimed to speak, permanently alienating people who have spent their lives feeling voiceless and powerless.

"Roots in the Rubble," by George Monbiot. Originally published in *The Guardian*, June 29, 2016. www.guardian.co.uk. Reprinted by permission of the author, George Monbiot. www.monbiot.com

Yes, the Brexit vote has empowered the most gruesome collection of schemers, misfits, liars, extremists and puppets British politics has produced in the modern era. It threatens to invoke a new age of demagoguery, a threat sharpened by the thought that if this can happen, so can Donald Trump. It has provoked a resurgence of racism and an economic crisis whose dimensions remain unknown. It jeopardises the living world, the NHS, peace in Ireland and the rest of the European Union. It promotes what the billionaire Peter Hargreaves gleefully anticipated as "fantastic insecurity."

But we're stuck with it. There isn't another option, unless you favour the years of limbo and chaos that would ensue from a continued failure to trigger Article 50. It's not just that we have no choice but to accept the result. We should embrace it and make of it what we can.

It's not as if the system that's now crashing around us was functioning. The vote could be seen as a self-inflicted wound, or it could be seen as the eruption of an internal wound, inflicted over many years by an economic oligarchy on the poor and the forgotten. The bogus theories on which our politics and economics are founded were going to collide with reality one day; the only questions were how and when.

Yes, the Brexit campaign was led by a political elite, funded by an economic elite and fueled by a media elite. Yes, popular anger was channelled towards undeserving targets—immigrants. But the vote was also a howl of rage against exclusion, alienation and remote authority. That is why the slogan "take back control" resonated. If the left can't work with this, what are we for?

So here is where we find ourselves. The economic system is not working, except for the likes of Philip Green. Neoliberalism has not delivered the meritocratic nirvana its theorists promised, but a rentiers' paradise, offering staggering returns to whoever grabs the castle first while leaving productive workers on the wrong side of the moat. The age of enterprise has become the age of unearned income; the age of the market, the age of market failure;

the age of opportunity, a steel cage of zero-hour contracts, precarity and surveillance.

The political system is not working. Whoever you vote for, the same people win, because where power claims to be is not where power is. Parliaments and councils embody paralysed force, gesture without motion, as the real decisions are taken elsewhere: by the money, for the money. Governments have actively conspired in this shift, negotiating fake trade treaties behind their voters' backs to prevent democracy from controlling corporate capital. Unreformed political funding ensures that parties have to listen to the rustle of notes before the bustle of votes. In Britain, these problems are compounded by an electoral system that ensures most votes don't count. This is why a referendum is almost the only means by which people can be heard, and why attempting to override it is a terrible idea.

Culture is not working. A worldview which insists that both people and place are fungible is inherently hostile to the need for belonging. For years we have been told that we do not belong, that we should shift out without complaint while others are shifted in to take our place. When the peculiarities of community and place are swept away by the tides of capital, all that's left is a globalised shopping culture, in which we engage with glazed passivity. Man was born free, and he is everywhere in chainstores.

In all these crises is opportunity. Opportunities to reject, connect and erect: to build from these ruins a system that works for the people of this country, rather than for an offshored elite that preys on insecurity. If it is true that Britain will have to renegotiate its trade treaties, is this not the best chance we've had in decades to contain corporate power? Of insisting that companies which operate here must offer proper contracts, share their profits, cut their emissions and pay their taxes? Is it not a chance to regain control of the public services slipping from our grasp?

How will politics in this sclerotised nation change without a maelstrom? In this chaos we can, if we are quick and clever, find a chance to strike a new contract: proportional representation, real

Brexit's Impact on the Eurozone

British people voted Thursday to leave the European Union after 43 years of membership. The decision chiefly affects the UK, but it will also reverberate well beyond its borders.

In the eurozone, we can distinguish between near-term and medium-term Brexit impacts of macro and political nature. The near-term macro implications are likely to be contained, though they are not insignificant. Eurozone exports to the UK are around 13% of total exports. If we estimate that UK GDP drops by 1%–1.5% over the next 12 months due to the decision to leave the EU, this would translate to a GDP shock for the eurozone on the order of 0.1%. This would come on top of a hit from tighter financial conditions and lower confidence. This latter effect on GDP is harder to quantify, but we would estimate it to be around 0.2%. In total, the shock might be around 0.3%, modest but not irrelevant for an economy where underlying growth is close to 1.25%. This additional shock to an already fragile recovery means that the European Central Bank may need to add yet again to its already aggressive quantitative easing program.

There may also be some longer-term macro consequences for the eurozone, but these are hard to assess at this early stage. The eurozone runs a trade surplus with the UK and to the extent that trade conditions worsen post EU renegotiations, this could be negative for the region. Against that, some of the foreign direct investment previously directed to the UK on the grounds that it was an EU member may be diverted into other EU countries.

Macro effects aside, the key spillovers into the eurozone from the UK vote are likely to be political. Market participants are already romancing the idea that similar referenda may be called elsewhere in the EU. In the near term, these don't seem likely, as populist euroskeptic parties are currently in opposition across the EU and therefore not likely to garner enough support in parliament to trigger such consultations. In some countries – such as Italy, the Netherlands and Poland—the population can make petitions for referenda, but legal limitations make petitions for votes on international treaties unlikely to succeed.

— "Brexit's Impact on the Eurozone," by Nicola Mai, PIMCO, June 24, 2016.

devolution and a radical reform of campaign finance to ensure that millionaires can never again own our politics.

Remote authority has been rejected, so let's use this moment to root our politics in a common celebration of place, to fight the epidemic of loneliness and rekindle common purpose, transcending the tensions between recent and less-recent immigrants (which means everyone else). In doing so, we might find a language in which liberal graduates can talk with the alienated people of Britain, rather than at them.

But most importantly, let's address the task that the left and centre have catastrophically neglected: developing a political and economic philosophy fit for the 21st Century, rather than repeatedly microwaving the leftovers of the 20th (neoliberalism and Keynesianism). If the history of the last 80 years tells us anything, it's that little changes without a new and feracious framework of thought. And when it arrives, everything changes. Much of my work over the next few months will be to assess what's on offer and try to identify and promote the best ideas.

So yes, despair and rage and curse: there are reasons enough to do so. But then raise your eyes to where hope lies.

VIEWPOINT 5

Reaction and Revolution

Jacob Høi Jensen

In the following viewpoint, Jacob Høi Jensen, who works for SKAT, the Danish tax authority, writes: "Brexit as a phenomenon provides an important window into how reaction as a political philosophy will be translated into an actual political program." In other words, Brexit voters meant to signal their discontent with the political and economic situation in the UK, but the causes and consequences of that dour reality are a political tangle. Leavers want economic independence, but the UK thrives on its ability to attract foreign capital because of its access to the EU's common market. Likewise, many voters bristled at the UK's having to adopt EU policies, but now Parliament will have to slog through the muddy process of converting EU law into UK law, revising and repealing as they go.

In his recent meditation on the role of reactionary ideas in politics, *The Shipwrecked Mind*, Mark Lilla provides a provocative and profound interpretation of political reaction. "The reactionary mind is a shipwrecked mind," he writes, "Where others see the river of time flowing as it always has, the reactionary sees the debris of paradise drifting past his eyes. He is time's exile. The revolutionary sees the radiant future invisible to others and it electrifies him. The reactionary, immune to modern lies, sees the past in all its splendor and he too is electrified."[1] In other words, reactionaries are of a similar ilk to revolutionaries; both mindsets draw their energy and values from "historical imaginings." For

"Past Imperfect: The Brexit Gamble," by Jacob Høi Jensen, EuropeNow, April 1, 2017.

the revolutionary, the prospect of a Marxist utopia in which class antagonisms have been overcome allows him or her to dismiss our liberal-democratic age as a mere stepping stone, a temporary phenomenon that is supposed to give way to a better future. For the reactionary, on the other hand, history has simply gone too far. The "well-ordered state where people who know their place live in harmony and submit to tradition and their God,"[2] has been dislodged by a chaotic, corrupt, and frivolous society which, if left intact, is bound to come to an end in an apocalyptic fashion. As the term "historical imaginings" suggests, however, the visions put forth by both mindsets are grounded in myths rather than reality. They rely on a combination of romanticized imagery and doomsaying in order to condemn the present.

Nowhere has this delicate relationship between reaction and revolution come more to the fore than in the United Kingdom's decision to withdraw from the European Union (EU). During the campaign leading up to the referendum, the Leave Camp—spearheaded by the likes of Boris Johnson, Michael Gove, and Nigel Farage—tirelessly invoked the past as a preferable alternative to the present. Under the slogan of "let's take back control," the Leave Camp promoted an image of the United Kingdom as a once great nation now encumbered by the shackles of the bureaucratic Leviathan that is the EU. Theresa May, though a supporter of the Remain Camp during the campaign, was quick to latch on to the Leave Camp's rhetoric after she assumed the position of Prime Minister. During her keynote speech on the final day of the Conservative Party's annual conference, which took place two and a half months after the referendum, May confidently stated that as a result of Brexit, the United Kingdom was going "to become, once more, a fully sovereign and independent country."[3] The implications of these statements are clear; only by once again becoming a fully sovereign country will the UK be able to rediscover its true glory.

Ever since the referendum took place, the British government has had to come to terms with the fact that while promoting nostalgia for a glorified past may prove an effective strategy for wooing voters, it is next to useless as a foundation for coherent and effective politics. By dismissing the EU as some kind of foreign entity that has done little more for the UK than burden it with absurd laws, the Brexiteers may discover that they have engaged in a Faustian gambit in which they have sacrificed complexity for the sake of winning the referendum. Consequently, they now find themselves having to explain why Brexit might be a slightly more complicated process than they promised. The truth is that the EU is so entangled with the legal, economic, and political fabric of the UK that the process of Brexit will necessarily lead to nothing less than an upheaval of the modern British state as we know it. Such a development will not lead to the a return of the glamourized pre-EU UK that the Brexiteers dream of, however, but rather an entirely different being.

Consider the economic consequences of a hard Brexit that will take Britain out of the EU's single market and customs union. For Brexiteers, such a step would represent an economic emancipation of their country, a development that would allow British businesses to flourish in the absence of arbitrary EU regulation, and for the UK itself to strike trade deals with non-EU member states without having to rely on the EU. The reality, however, is that the UK economy is more dependent than ever on its membership of the EU. For the past couple of decades, the British economy has essentially been built around a strategy in which the country's favorable financial and legal environment, combined with its access to the EU, has been used to attract foreign capital on an unprecedented scale. This influx has resulted in what has been described as the "death of British business,"[4] a situation in which British companies have either become increasingly uncompetitive, or disappeared entirely. As Simon Head has argued, "what has saved Britain from relegation to the European lower echelons—to the level of Italy, Spain, or worse—has been the pursuit over several decades of an economic strategy that has encouraged global corporations in both manufacturing and financial services to come to the UK and fill the British business vacuum."[5] Once the UK loses access to the single market, foreign companies will have little reason to invest in the British economy—a warning that has been put forth by numerous countries, including Japan[6] and the US[7]—and as a result of decades of reliance on foreign business, British companies will not be strong enough to fill the vacuum left behind.

The legal ramifications of Brexit seem no less daunting. Theresa May has set out plans for a "Great Repeal Bill" to be included in the next Queen's Speech. While there is next to no information available regarding the specifics of such a bill, it seems that it will be intended for removing the European Communities Act 1972 (ECA), the mechanism by which EU law is brought into UK law. Such a bill would convert existing EU-based laws into domestic legislation, thereby allowing Parliament to "amend, repeal and improve any law it chooses."[8] Such an act would constitute nothing less than the "greatest legal transplant on these isles since the reception of Roman law in Scotland in the late Middle Ages."[9] Disentangling and assessing 43 years of legal integration will occupy the British parliament and civil service for years. To further complicate matters, the ECA and other primary legislation implementing EU laws are incorporated into the devolution states in Scotland, Wales, and Northern Ireland. Consequently, any attempt to convert existing EU law into domestic British law will necessarily touch upon devolved matters, an action that is bound to set Westminster on a collision course with devolved assemblies in Northern Ireland and Scotland. Considering the fact that Scotland voted in favour of the UK staying in the EU by 62 percent to 38 percent, such a conflict could ultimately have fatal consequences for the Union.[10]

In their desperate attempt to promote a vision of a United Kingdom, which is based on a glorified and nostalgic interpretation of the past, Brexiteers have unleashed a process that risks upending the legal, economic, and political foundations of the modern UK. Furthermore, they have yet to offer a coherent and realistic vision of what will replace it. As reactionary politics are bound to continue to play an integral role in 2017—the inauguration of Donald Trump as the 45th President of the United States will take place in January, Francois Fillon is all but certain to face the National Front's Marie Le Pen in the second round of the French Presidential Election on April 23, and the *Alternative für Deutshland* party is currently projected to win 15 percent of the vote in the German Federal Election in September, thereby becoming the first radical-right party to enter the Bundestag since the Constitution of the German Democratic Republic was created in 1949[11]—Brexit as a phenomenon provides an important window into how reaction as a political philosophy will be translated into an actual political program. Judging by the results so far, reactionary political forces may find it easier to dismantle existing political institutions than they will replacing them.

References

1. Lilla, Mark. *The Shipwrecked Mind: On Political Reaction*. New York: New York Review, 2016. Print. Page XXI.

2. Ibid.

3. The *Independent*. (2016). Read Theresa May's keynote speech to the Conservative conference in full. [online] Available at: http://www.independent.co.uk/news/uk/politics/theresa-may-speech-tory-conference-2016-in-full-transcript-a7346171.html [Accessed 25 Nov. 2016].

4. Head, S. (2016). *The Death of British Business*. [online] The New York Review of Books. Available at: http://www.nybooks.com/daily/2016/10/18/brexit-death-of-british-business/ [Accessed 26 Nov. 2016].

5. Ibid.

6. Edwards, J. (2016). *You should read Japan's Brexit note to Britain — it's brutal*. [online] *Business Insider*. Available at: http://www.businessinsider.com/japan-brexit-note-to-britain-2016-9?r=UK&IR=T&IR=T [Accessed 2 Jan. 2017].

7. Moshinsky, B. (2016). *US business lobby to UK: We need 'unfettered access' to Europe*. [online] Business Insider. Available at: http://www.businessinsider.com/us-chamber-of-commerce-warning-over-brexit-2016-10?r=UK&IR=T&IR=T [Accessed 3 Jan. 2017].

8. Reuters. (2016). *Highlights: British PM May on Brexit, Article 50 and trade*. [online] Available at: http://www.reuters.com/article/us-britain-eu-may-speech-idUSKCN1220LM [Accessed 26 Nov. 2016].

9. Murkens, Jo. 2016. "The Great 'Repeal' Act Will Leave Parliament Sidelined And Disempowered". *LSE – London School of Economics*. http://blogs.lse.ac.uk/

brexit/2016/10/21/the-great-repeal-act-will-leave-parliament-sidelined-and-disempowered/.

10. BBC News. (2016). *EU referendum: Scotland backs Remain as UK votes Leave – BBC News.* [online] Available at: http://www.bbc.com/news/uk-scotland-scotland-politics-36599102 [Accessed 2 Jan. 2017].

11. Arzheimer, K. (2016). *Look ahead to 2017: The German federal election. [online] European Politics and Policy.* Available at: http://blogs.lse.ac.uk/europpblog/2016/12/31/look-ahead-to-2017-the-german-federal-election/ [Accessed 2 Jan. 2017].

VIEWPOINT 6

Brexit and Globalization

Italo Colantone and Piero Stanig

The vote for Brexit was a watershed moment in European politics. This column by Bocconi University professors Italo Colantone and Piero Stanig, who teach economics and political science, respectively, investigates the causal drivers of differences in support for the Leave campaign across UK regions. Globalization in the form of the "Chinese import shock" is found to be a key driver of regional support for Brexit, according to the authors. The results suggest that policies are needed that help to redistribute the benefits of globalization across society.

The success of the "Leave" campaign in the Brexit referendum of June 2016 was probably the single most important event in European politics in the past two decades. A good deal of debate and analysis has followed the referendum, mostly in the form of blog posts and articles in the press. A number of empirical regularities have been established, both with respect to individual-level determinants of Leave votes, and in terms of social and economic conditions that correlate with support for Brexit across geographic areas. In particular, there is evidence that UK regions characterised by declining shares of manufacturing employment, lower real wage growth, and increasing income inequality voted systematically more to leave the EU (e.g. Becker et al. 2016, Bell and Machin 2016, Colantone and Stanig 2016a,

Clarke and Whittaker 2016, Darvas 2016, Langella and Manning 2016, Menon and Salter 2016).

In a recent paper, we show that the Chinese import shock is a key causal driver of differences in support for Leave across regions (Colantone and Stanig 2016b). In particular, regions that have been more exposed to the recent surge of manufacturing imports from China, due to their historical industry specialisation, show systematically higher Leave vote shares. We claim that this causal effect is driven by the displacement determined by globalisation in the absence of effective compensation of its losers. In that respect, our analysis addresses the fundamental determinants of divergence in regional performance emphasised by previous contributions.

The Chinese Import Shock

We compute a region-specific measure for the exposure to Chinese imports following the methodology developed by Autor et al. (2013). This measure combines national-level import data at the industry level with regional data on the pre-sample composition of employment by industries. The intuition is straightforward: different regions have been more or less exposed to the Chinese shock depending on their ex ante industry specialisation. In particular, larger shocks are attributed to regions in which more workers were initially employed in the manufacturing sector. However, for a given overall share of manufacturing workers, the shock is stronger for regions in which more workers were originally employed in industries for which Chinese imports have increased the most over time, for example textiles or electronic goods. We compute the import shock for a total of 167 NUTS-3 British regions. We consider the growth in Chinese imports between 1990 and 2007, and measure regional industry specialisation in 1989.[1] Trade data are from Eurostat (Comext), while employment data are from the UK Office for National Statistics.

Figure 1 shows the variation in the strength of the import shock across more aggregated NUTS-2 regions, for convenience of exposition. At the NUTS-3 level, the variable we employ has an average value of 0.32. This corresponds to a growth in imports from China by 320 real euros per worker, computed as the five-year moving average over the sample. The region with the lowest shock is Camden and City of London (0.06), while the region with the largest shock is Leicester (0.75).

Figure 1. Map of the Chinese import shock across NUTS-2 regions

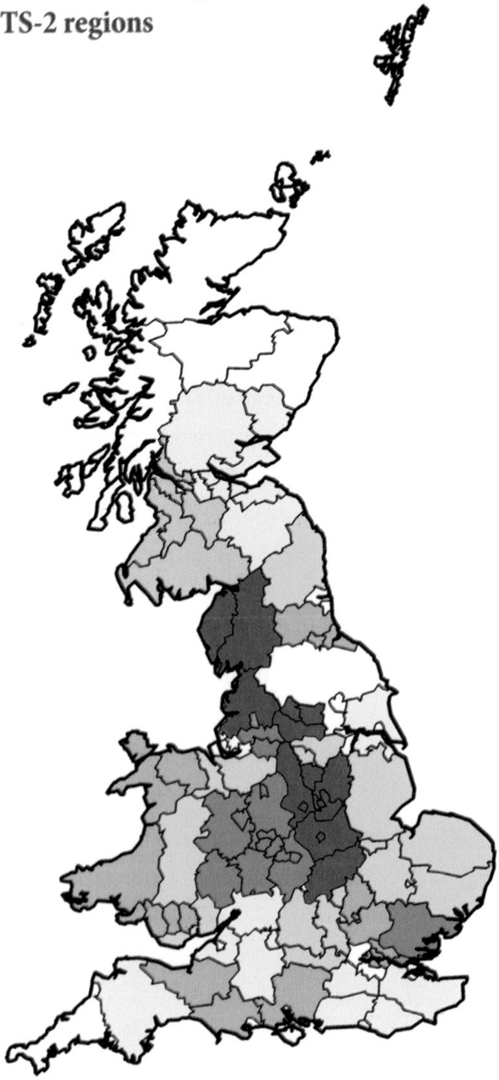

Darker shades correspond to stronger import shock

The Effect of Import Competition on Leave Votes

To investigate the impact of import competition on support for Brexit, we regress Leave vote shares at the NUTS-3 regional level on the Chinese import shock of the region. We include in the specification fixed effects for the corresponding NUTS-1 macro regions. This allows us to account for any confounder that affects similarly all the NUTS-3 areas in a macro region—for example, a different political culture in Scotland, which is one of the 12 NUTS-1 British regions we consider. Importantly, to account for the role of immigration, we include in our regressions both the stock of foreign born residents in the population, and the recent arrival rate of immigrants, both measured at the NUTS-3 level in 2015.

To account for the possible endogeneity of the import shock, in line with several earlier studies we instrument Chinese imports to the UK by using Chinese imports to the US (e.g. Autor et al. 2013, Colantone et al. 2015, Bloom et al. 2016). This instrumentation strategy aims to capture the variation in Chinese imports to the UK that is driven by changes in supply conditions in China, rather than by potentially endogenous domestic factors in Britain.

We find that Leave vote shares are systematically higher in regions that have witnessed larger import shocks. Specifically, a one standard deviation increase in the strength of the import shock at the regional level leads to an increase by two percentage points in support for the Leave option. Moreover, if we compare a NUTS-3 region at the 10th percentile of the distribution of the import shock (Cardiff and Vale of Glamoran) with a region at the 90th percentile (Gwent Valleys) within the same NUTS-1 macro region (Wales), these are expected to differ by four and a half percentage points in their support for Leave. In fact, the actual difference was 16 percentage points.

We do not find any evidence that immigration is related to more support for Leave. If anything, we detect a negative correlation between the share of foreign-born residents in the population and Leave shares. All our findings are robust to controlling for the unemployment rate in the region, for the share of high-skill workers, and for the share of agriculture in regional GDP.

Individual-level Evidence

We complement the regional-level analysis with regressions exploiting individual-level data on vote intentions, sourced from the British Election Study (Wave 8). We have data on a total of 31,409 respondents, surveyed in May–June 2016 (just before the referendum). For each individual we have information on vote intentions, as well as on demographic characteristics, education, labour market status, type of occupation, and attitudes towards immigration. We regress a dummy for voting Leave against the import competition shock in the region of residence, controlling both for the immigration variables and for NUTS-1 fixed effects. In addition, we control for age, gender, and education of the respondent.

Consistently with the regional-level evidence, we find that the Chinese import shock has a positive effect on the propensity to vote for Leave. Moreover, in line with existing evidence, older and male respondents are more likely to support Leave, while higher educational attainment reduces the probability of voting for Brexit. On the other hand, we do not detect any significant association between immigration and support for the Leave option.

Working with individual-level data allows us to investigate how the effect of import competition varies across voters depending on their labour market status and occupation. We do so by interacting the import shock with dummies for specific categories of voters. Our results suggest that the effect of import competition is not confined to a specific group of individuals who might be more directly affected by the shock—for example, the unemployed. Rather, the import shock seems to have a very similar impact across the whole population, and even for service workers, whose jobs are not directly affected by manufacturing imports from China.

By and large, our evidence suggests that voters are reacting to the import shock in a sociotropic way, responding to the general economic situation of their region, regardless of their specific condition.

Import Competition and Attitudes Towards Immigration

We have not found evidence that higher levels of immigration are significantly related to higher support for Leave. And yet, dissatisfaction with immigration has been identified as one of the most important self-reported reasons for voters supporting the Leave option (Ipsos MORI 2016, Lord Ashcroft 2016). How can we reconcile these pieces of evidence? In our individual-level data, we find evidence that negative attitudes towards immigration are themselves determined by stronger exposure to Chinese imports, more than by the extent of immigration in the region of residence. Overall, regardless of the self-reported reasons for voting Leave, concerns with immigration might be better understood as a scapegoat for a malaise that has more structural economic origins. These are related to large scale economic transformations that inflict disproportionate losses on some sectors of society.

Conclusion

Globalisation, and in particular the Chinese import shock, was a key driver of the vote for Brexit. While free trade has generated significant welfare gains for advanced economies such as the UK, the distribution of these gains has been highly unequal. This has left some social groups and, importantly, some geographic areas, much worse off. Our results suggest that redistribution policies that spread the benefits of globalisation across society are crucial to ensure that globalisation itself is sustainable in the long run.

References

Autor, D, D Dorn and G Hanson (2013) "The China syndrome: Local labor market effects of import competition in the United States", *American Economic Review*, 103: 2121-2168.

Becker, S O, F Fetzer and D Novy (2016) "Who voted for Brexit? A comprehensive district-level analysis", CAGE Working Paper 305, October.

Bell, B and S Machin (2016) "Brexit and wage inequality", Mimeo, London School of Economics and Political Science.

Bloom, N, M Draca and J Van Reenen (2016) "Trade-induced technical change: The impact of Chinese imports on innovation, IT and productivity", *Review of Economic Studies,* 83: 87-117.

Clarke, S and M Whittaker (2016), "The importance of place: Explaining the characteristics underpinning the Brexit vote across different parts of the UK", Resolution Foundation, London.

Colantone, I, R Crinò and L Ogliari (2015) "The hidden cost of globalization: Import competition and mental distress", CEPR, Discussion Paper 10874.

Colantone, I and P Stanig (2016a) "The real reason the UK voted for Brexit? Jobs lost to Chinese competition", *The Washington Post,* 7 July.

Colantone, I and P Stanig (2016b) "Global competition and Brexit", BAFFI CAREFIN Centre Research Paper 2016-44, November.

Darvas, Z (2016) "Brexit should be a wake up call in the fight against inequality", London School of Economics and Political Science, London.

Ipsos MORI (2016) "Britain remains split as nine in ten say they would not change their referendum vote", Ipsos MORI, London.

Langella, M and A Manning (2016) "Who voted Leave: The characteristics of individuals mattered, but so did those of local areas", London School of Economics and Political Science, London.

Lord Ashcroft (2016) "How the United Kingdom voted on Thursday and why", Lord Ashcroft Polls, London.

Menon, A and J P Salter (2016) "Brexit: Initial reflections", *International Affairs,* 92: 1297–1318.

Chapter 3

What's Next for the UK, the EU, and the World?

Preface

It's easy to look at Brexit as an isolated incident, the backlash of a slim majority in a divided nation that has always been touchy about surrendering sovereignty. But, as the viewpoints in this final chapter make clear, Brexit did indeed reverberate around the world. It was a kind of prophecy. So long as the educated were at odds with the unschooled, and the unschooled were plied with propaganda, and propaganda invoked suspicion of immigrants, and those immigrants felt threatened by their new compatriots, then the conditions existed for Brexitesque hostilities.

On the home front, Brexit had a discordant effect on Scotland, where nearly two-thirds of voters favored remaining in the EU. Some have wondered whether Brexit might prompt Scotland to embark on a new bid for independence from the UK but, as John Curtice observes in Viewpoint 4, such speculation may be premature. Farther afield, several of the authors in this chapter reflect on the parallels between the Leave camp's victory and Donald Trump's election as US president. Both seemed to ride a wave of populism (populism being an amorphous ideology—often bound to an extreme form of patriotic superiority, and disdain for global cooperation, known as nationalism—that pits the pure plebeian against the corrupt elite).

In the first viewpoint in this chapter, Alistair Campbell tackles the symmetry between Brexit and Trump head on and tries to suss out how both came to pass and what they mean for the future. Later, Jonathan Gatehouse, Charlie Gillis, and Sally Hayden explore the likelihood that other nations may copy Britain's break with the EU, and Andrew Hines muses on the etymological significance of the Brexit debate, arguing it has called into question the very meaning of the word "democracy."

Viewpoint 1

First Comes Brexit, Then Comes Trump, Then Comes…

Alastair Campbell

In the following viewpoint, author, journalist and former press secretary for Prime Minister Tony Blair Alastair Campbell gives his no-holds-barred take on what Brexit and Donald Trump mean for the world, noting that these polarizing events have "confirmed that we are indeed now in the era of post-truth politics." Campbell, who has also written for GQ, Esquire, *the* Mirror, *and the* Times of London, *adds that the only recourse is to "never stop calling out the lies and the excesses."*

Yesterday I made a speech to a conference organised by Fremantle Media, the independent production company that has given us such delights—depending on your taste—as Pop Idol, The Price is Right, and The Bill. They wanted me to talk about Trump, Brexit, the rise of populism, and what it all said about politics and media now and in the future. On arrival at The Grove in Hertfordshire, I discovered that what I thought was a fifty-minute slot was just twenty-five, and some of that was for Q and A. So I got out the red pen and set to slashing. It seemed to go well enough, but here, for those who don't mind a bit of long-form, is the fifty-minute version.

"What Trump, Brexit and the rise of populism say about politics and media now and in the future," by Alastair Camphell, Alastair Campbell, December 8, 2016. Reprinted by Permission.

I do like an event where I get a good clear brief, based on clear questions emailed over to me well in advance to give me time to think.

So here goes with the questions you asked me to answer.

What will the Trump presidency look like?
That one is easy. F--k knows.

What are his priorities?
Also easy. No idea. They change from tweet to tweet. Today it seems to be the replacement of Air Force One.

What do we know he's definitely going to do?
Normally it is what the elected politician campaigned on. So … *Lock her up*. No, he's changed his mind, Hillary is a wonderful woman. *Build a wall.* Apparently it is going to be a fence now. *Drain the swamp*. Now the Goldman Sachs guy is in the treasury, several of Trump's billionaire pals are in the Cabinet, and there is a confusing mix of politics and business, including taking his daughter to meetings with PMs so she can tweet pictures and tell the world where to buy her bangle.

Who is on his team and what does this mean?
Bannon for one. It means the alt-right is normalized and part of the mainstream. As yet he still has no Secretary of State, and given the row over Taiwan I kind of feel he may be needing one quite soon.

Who are his allies globally?
Nigel Farage, Piers Morgan and Vladimir Putin, and none strike me as US Secretary of State material. It makes that other trio of Johnson, Fox and Davis look like Abraham Lincoln's team of rivals … with China, it is fair to say, he has made a bad start. But rival superpowers apart, he knows other countries will want to get close. Power attracts power.

What is Trump like and what can we expect from his leadership?

You know the answer to the first part—you saw the horror show as much as I did—and the second part you know you don't know.

Next you asked me about the Global Implications of The New Populism. **What is it? What is the emerging new world order and what does it mean? Why is populism becoming so attractive around the world? How we can expect the world to change—what is under threat?** Nothing much—just the whole of Western civilization and the future of the planet maybe. What could go wrong with a leader who said climate change was a Chinese hoax? What could go wrong if two leaders like Putin and Trump went man to man, fell out, got the willies out and neither would back down?

What should we be watching out for in 2017?

My own hope is that we wake up to the disaster that is Brexit and change course, and Trump's win turns out to be the most spectacular example of Fake News yet. Instead we shall look to see how Le Pen fares in France and Wilders in Holland. We shall in the main be praying Angela Merkel survives to win another term. And we will be watching to see who or what can tame Trump.

Certainly we are living through remarkable change. Recently I published volume 5 of my diaries, which cover 2003-05. Theresa May appears once. Jeremy Corbyn not at all. Trump not at all. The word Brexit did not exist. Now here we are, a tumultuous referendum come and gone, David Cameron—come and gone; a leader of the Labour Party seen as unelectable by many but unassailable in the Party, and Trump seen as unelectable by most members of the human race, but now president elect of the most powerful country on earth.

"Love trumps hate" goes the slogan. Oh yeah? Not in the populist age.

Feeling would seem to trump reason.

Anger trumps logic.

Direction trumps detail.

Simple messages trump complex arguments.

And the Oxford English Dictionary chose 'post-truth' as its new word of the year.

Hillary's campaign wasn't bad, you know. Experience. Knowledge of how the world works. Detail and understanding of complicated policy briefs home and abroad. Stability in a time of turmoil. Continuity from a widely respected President she had served closely and well.

These are all, to anyone involved in post war democratic politics, positives. And up against what? Someone with no political, diplomatic or military experience. A proven liar, sexist, racist, narcissist, misogynist and even—when it came to things like demonising whole races or religions, or saying he would only accept the result if he won, and lock up his opponent when he did—with tinges of proto-fascist in there too.

So what did he do well?

He turned her strengths into weaknesses, and his own weaknesses into strengths—not in the eyes of most of the political, diplomatic and mainstream media classes, who became ever more convinced of his awfulness, but in the eyes of the people he decided he needed to win, for whom the reaction of these elites seemed to bolster his appeal. For experience, read Washington insider, part of, and indeed symbol of, the system that needs to change. The first woman President? That excited liberals. Helped by Bernie Sanders, who started with the "creature of Goldman Sachs" thing, and by the email "scandal," he turned her into something close to a witch. Does anyone here know what she did wrong with her emails? In the end it didn't matter. No fire, lots and lots of smoke.

As for him, for billionaire businessman who won't reveal his taxes, read smart success story. For a few Chapter 11 bankruptcies along the way, read resilience. For temperamental unpredictable firecracker, read someone who tells it like it is and says the things nobody else dare. Hillary's supporters projected her as the perfect President. Trump supporters liked his flaws.

Also, his message was clearer. *Make America Great Again*. It is active not static like *Stronger Together*. It is a call to arms suggesting a better future. But it also relates back to what people can be made to think is a better past. *Make* says the future. *Again* summons up the past. *Stronger Together* says Now, trapped in time ... Hillary seems to have forgotten the Fleetwood Mac anthem of her husband's first win ... *Don't stop thinking about tomorrow*. We had a similar theme in 1997, *Things can only get better*, remember. They did by the way.

Trump was change. He turned Hillary into continuity. People wanted change, at least enough of them did to get him over the line. She won the popular vote but he won the election by winning where he needed to.

To those struggling in the rust belt, there *was* a better past, the good old days seemed real. "Take back control" in the referendum was a similar message. "Back" is the key word there ... let's restore something we have lost because of others. Brussels. Immigrants. Globalisation. Elites. All easy targets. Then wrap in a few lies about NHS spending, and you're away.

Brexit and Trump focused, with non-conventional politicians in the lead, pretending they were anti-elitist, on what a brand would call forgotten consumers. What is remarkable about this in the States is that the Clintons built their rise on an understanding of these people. Bill was of them. It's incredible that a spoilt, rich, inherited wealth billionaire should now seem to understand them and claim to represent them better, but he made them think he did. What is more he used methods that our conventional wisdoms felt would backfire. This exposed the level of disconnect. Likewise with Brexit, the Big Lie that this was about taking on the elite—an old Etonian like Johnson, a City trader like Farage, media barons like Murdoch, Dacre, the Barclays—the elite of the Brexit Lie Machine.

Media change is important here. When reality TV first became a thing, one Christmas at Tessa Jowell's house, she, her family and mine were all getting into Pop Idol or X Factor or one of those. I'm afraid I have never much liked any of them. Tessa was obsessed with a binman called Andy and kept pinging her phone to vote for him. And when I said you are playing with fire, they said I was a grumpy old man who didn't understand the modern world. But I think I did.

To millions, voting in those entertainment shows seemed to matter at least as much as voting in elections. The increasingly nihilist papers would give you ten reasons to vote for singer X or comedian Y, made into instant celebrities by dint of being on the show. The same papers would tell you day after day ten reasons not to get involved in politics where they are all the same, in it for themselves, blah blah blah.

Trump is the perfect symbol for this change. An entertainer. A storyteller narrating his favourite subject—himself. If he spoke, the media felt compelled to cover it because they knew the public wanted to see him … see the next episode … what will he do next … mock a disabled person, insult a race, fight with a war hero, whip up anger against journalists in a pen, hit new lows in the attacks on Hillary, make policy promises no serious person believes will happen …? He got $4.2billion worth of free air time in the US, and media companies the world over need to reflect on their role in his rise. Oh, and guess who is on Question Time again tomorrow? Farage. I don't know why he doesn't just take over from David Dimbleby.

Even a few years ago, the Trump strategy wouldn't have worked. It worked now, in the reality TV/ social media world that is transforming our politics in ways which Trump clearly fathomed better than Hillary, the media, the pollsters, the bookies. In my day, you needed consistency of message. But Trump's inconsistency and unpredictability became part of the appeal. He was like a one man soap opera, and the next episode was likely to fascinate and shock even more. And we all thought there was no way the American people would fall for this. But they did. Someone once said politics was showbiz for ugly people. In Trump the two have fused. He even tweeted out, a week after he won, that only he knew who 'the contestants' were for the top jobs. In the reality TV age, the reality TV President. In the post-truth world, the post-truth President.

There is a very interesting social media analytical tool called EMOTIVE, which correctly predicted the outcome based on an analysis of the emotional depth of the many millions of tweets the two candidates were generating. It can analyse thousands of tweets a second to extract from each tweet a direct expression of one of eight basic emotions: anger, disgust, fear, happiness, sadness, surprise, shame and confusion. It was first developed in 2013 to predict whether another riot could happen in London. It accurately predicted our 2015 election.

During the three weeks leading up to the vote, Trump led in terms of the consistency of the emotions he was arousing. What the model is seeking out is not numerical support so much as consistency in the emotional response. The more emotions fluctuate, the greater the uncertainty towards a candidate, and the fewer votes the model predicts a candidate is going to get. The model does not concern itself with the direction of the emotion or put value on one emotion over another—because an emotion such as anger can be positive or negative.

Another plank of populism is the demonization of people who know what they are talking about, their reason made irrelevant alongside people's anger. Just as in Brexit "we have had enough of experts," (copyright Michael Gove) so in the US all voices of conventional wisdom were dismissed by those forgotten consumers Trump was chasing.

So anger was the key. He needed to express anger as a way of showing he got the anger of people. It became a virtuous circle for him. *Say* they are angry. *Show* he is angry. *Make* them more angry. And make them believe that the old ways and the old people who had been around for years wouldn't be able to fix the reasons for their anger. Only he would. Saviour time.

Meanwhile in the media and political bubbles we all persuaded each other we knew what was going on. As the date neared I found myself increasingly emailing and calling my US friends—some working for Hillary—saying please tell me this isn't happening. No way, they said, all of them, without exception, including on polling day. She will win. Fret not.

It was strange—during our referendum campaign in June, every time I ventured out of the UK I was met with people from other countries stunned that we were even thinking of leaving the EU. Then I would come back home and hear so many people here—particularly outside London—who were determined that it is exactly what we should do. It has been the same for Americans travelling abroad in recent months—nobody outside America (and Putin's Russia) seemed to want Trump. But Trump is what the world now has. The people who create the conventional wisdoms —the political, economic and media class if you like, all in their own bubbles, barely speak to the kind of people who swung it for Brexit and for Trump. And when they do there is a disconnent.

Conventional wisdom says don't go full frontal on the media. Trump did. Did it harm him? No. Because the landscape has changed so much.

24 news and social media have changed journalism out of all recognition. People just move on. All about impact. Straight to comment. Fusion of news and comment. It's easy to see why this happened—papers not merely in competition with each other but with all other parts of the landscape. Fake news now a reality in this post-truth world.

And campaigning which disregards facts in favour of emotion having proved successful in the most followed democracy of all, we can expect more of it, and the media will have to adapt.

Also, be honest, what has most of our broadcast media become? Journalists talking to each other about what other journalists say. Commentators reviewing on TV what they and others have said in the papers. Newsreaders telling you what commentators are saying on twitter. Media outlets with more space to fill and fewer journalists to fill it with. This is tailor made for a Trump or a Brexit campaign, storming social media, overwhelming mainstream media.

Most reporting is done from the desk and less and less on the ground. The antennae picking up and understanding social change are less alive. Easy talk is prioritised over news-gathering because it's cheaper—but not necessarily well informed. And in elections, it has spawned an over-reliance on telephone and online polls—now proven unreliable, yet still relied upon to fill the space.

Also, again be honest, media has become a largely white, middle-class profession with fewer ways into the business for those without connections. This reinforces insularity of views, attitudes and approaches—not simply along political lines but social lines of class, region, education.

As traditional media has struggled, social networks have grown. But through the lens of these two campaigns, Trump and Brexit, their shortcomings are clear. Facebook now a planet of misinformation, Twitter a planet of abuse and division. Mark Zuckerberg happy to take credit for two million more people registering to vote, but shunting aside any responsibility for monetized fake news sites which add to his power and wealth. And the power of algorithms, which so few of us even begin, or even try, to understand, creating sealed echo chambers where we are seldom challenged by views we disagree with –further driving polarisation. Angela Merkel made a fascinating speech recently in which she warned of the dangers posed by algorithms constantly pointing us all in the direction of views we already hold. I remember my daughter on the day after Cameron won … "but how did this happen? Everyone said Labour would win." No, everyone in *our* digital world did.

Obama advisor David Axelrod once said when Obama was defying the odds to beat Hillary for the nomination in 08, "conventional wisdoms are always wrong." But actually nearer the mark is that there is no conventional wisdom any more. There are just billions of people around the world and we all have our own world, our own view, our own bubbles.

So as Trump moved to make the sale, the Brexit comparisons were obvious. A divided country still healing from the scars of the global financial crisis for which working people felt they—and not those who caused the crisis—paid the price. A feeling that the pace of change was too fast and the system needed a kick up the backside to get the message. An anti-establishment and anti-politics and anti-mainstream media mood. The politics of identity being turned into the politics of blame and becoming centered on immigrants at one end of the social scale, vaguely defined elites at the other. Hugely complicated issues reduced to simple messages repeatedly hammered home by the campaign and endlessly ventilated on social media. And the reason I feel this is a scary time to be alive is because I see in all of the above—particularly with the possibility for the break-up of the EU—echoes of, and parallels with, the 1930s.

We had it confirmed that we are indeed now in the era of post-truth politics. Trump made statements that made the Johnson Red Bus lies look tame by comparison. He said and did so many things that would frankly have killed off any other candidate in the past. The "pussy grabbing" tape was but the most high profile as the campaign neared its close, when only FBI director James Comey saved him from further embarrassment.

But the forgotten consumers he was chasing saw someone saying what he—and maybe they—thought. An actor playing to their emotions. His "'locker room banter" defence was not seen as abuse of women but an attack on political correctness.

"I never said that," said Trump in one of the debates pushing back at his comments on climate change being a Chinese hoax. He did. It is on camera. Ten, twenty years ago that might have done for him. We saw similar here … Lies just accepted … The £350m a week for the NHS. The tens of millions of Turks flooding Britain. The end of the British army being nigh.

Populists the world over, not least in Europe, will take heart from this. The insurgent has an inbuilt advantage. The more noise you make the more people seem to listen. Making people laugh, or making them feel, is as important as making them think. Getting down and dirty, despite what Michelle Obama said about the need to stay high when your opponent goes low, seems to have won the day.

As for what Trump will do, is it not incredible that normally we complain if politicians *don't* do the things they said they would? With Trump, he is getting praise from the media, and we are breathing a sigh of relief, every time he looks like he *won't* do something he said he would. This is politics and democracy turned upside down.

The red bus liar-in-chief is now foreign secretary, and in interviews and debates the Brexit lies barely seem to get a mention. What happened to being held to account? He says during the campaign we need to vote Brexit to keep the evil Turks out of the EU. Then goes to Istanbul as Foreign Secretary to say we support Turkish accession to the EU. Post-truth politics indeed.

This makes it so much easier for the liars and the charlatans of our world if they can just move on without properly being held to account.

We pride ourselves on the strength of our democracies. But if this is the way our politics is going, how long before we are not really so much better than the Putin we all claim to say is worse? Is it not perhaps just a question of scale? There is a great book about Putin's Russia, by Peter Pomerantsev, called "Nothing is true and anything is possible." Invade a country, then say you haven't. Poison your enemies on the streets of London. Say you didn't. Bring down planes. Deny it. Interfere in elections abroad. Say it is a CIA lie. How fast has the world changed, that seeming direct Russian interference in the US elections actually created such little fuss?

And on fake news, Barack Obama made an interesting observation. "The new media ecosystem means everything is true and nothing is true." Perhaps he had also seen the Pomerantsev book. "An explanation of climate change from a Nobel Prize-winning physicist looks exactly the same on your Facebook page as the denial of climate change by somebody on the Koch brothers' payroll," the President went on. "'And the capacity to disseminate misinformation, wild conspiracy theories, to paint the opposition in wildly negative light without any rebuttal—that has accelerated in ways that much more sharply polarize the electorate and make it very difficult to have a common conversation."

Trump eyes Vladimir Putin not just with a certain admiration as a strongman leader, but with envy too. He sees a leader who can get more done when he has no real opposition, control of his Parliament, the media, civil society and all the other checks on power. This is the other worrying lesson to draw from the Obama years of gridlock—that democracies seem in some ways to operate at a disadvantage to non-democracies and pseudo democracies.

But if he had campaigned overtly for that kind of power, it is unlikely Trump would have made it. So, just as the Brexiteers had to do, he needed to dress himself up as the crusader for the common man, taking on the elites on behalf of those who felt powerless and left behind. Given who and what he is, it was of course a gigantic con, with many lies wrapped around it. But when people feel that they are powerless and left behind, a populist message and messenger will resonate far more powerfully than someone offering stability and continuity.

So what does it mean for how politics and campaigning now change. Most people, even at the top end of politics, are not gigantic personalities as he is. Most people wouldn't get away with it. Boris Johnson is the nearest parallel, but when push came to shove, the Tories decided he was not the guy. Theresa May, fair to say, is no Trump. We cannot see Merkel changing her ways, thankfully.

But Merkel is outstanding in the literal sense. She stands out, and long may she do so. Europe needs her right now. But what recent events have shown is that people are looking for insurgence, for disruption, and incremental won't do.

So does that mean we are doomed to see politics fought on the extremes, even if most people still live their lives close to the centre? It is certainly easier to do so from there.

It is not just about dumbing down. It is about the pace of events around us. It is about the death of journalism as a profession with real standards. It is about us being able to create our own media landscape.

Trump was there, present in all of our lives and minds for some time. Did people want HIM? Not so much when he started. But did they want what he was offering—change, disruption, yes. He was making the weather in a way that felt horribly tactical, but in the end it turned out to be a remarkable strategic success. Everything said Me not Her. Everything said Feeling not Reason. Everything said Big Change not Continuity.

There will be plenty of politicians hoping he is a one off, and plenty more aiming to learn and somehow adapt and follow. But will they have the nerve and the personality to emulate?

In the end this is about the public. We say we want politicians who tell us the truth. But do we? What were the American people looking for? A savior. Or someone to kick the system? What was Brexit about? As much about kicking the establishment as a thought through decision on the detail of an exit that will be as fraught and complicated as it is uncertain and dangerous.

Trump is going to be President. Brexit is likely to happen, even with most of our MPs and the loathed experts knowing it will be a disaster. Brexit means Brexit. And now that means it is going to be a 'red, white and blue Brexit,' says Mrs May, meaningless gibberish in the absence of a meaningful government strategy.

But remember this—just because something is happening doesn't mean we have to accept it is right. I am reminded of former tennis champion John McEnroe's brilliant observation "'show me a good loser and I'll show you a loser." Frankly there is too much good losing going on, and a lot for the losers on both sides of the Atlantic to get bad about.

Trump lost the popular vote by a fair old margin yet now conducts himself as though he speaks not just for the whole of America but the whole of the world. The Brexiteers won by a narrow margin, yet conduct debate as though the referendum means only one view is allowed. So Trump's chosen Ambassador for the UK, Farage, in this era of post truth politics, struts around the place insisting 17 million people voted to leave the single market when even those he campaigned with were clear at the time it meant nothing of the sort.

Here is where the losers need to stop feeling they have to pander to the winners, and keep calling them out on their lies past and present. And here, both with Trump and with Brexit our Prime Minister needs to take a lead in shaping a more nuanced response.

Accepted, Trump has been elected leader of the most powerful country in the world and Mrs May must develop a relationship with him. But pandering to rudeness and narcissism does not constitute a foreign policy. She should study carefully the words with which Angela Merkel greeted Trump's election. She cited shared values, not least to remind the Americans these were as much their values as hers. Mrs May has looked by contrast somewhat desperate, briefing out of her phone call with Trump that he had confirmed his commitment to a "special relationship"—so special (sic) that she was the eleventh leader he called and the transcript subsequently revealed his "invitation" to visit was little more than "let me know if you're ever popping by." Then came the notion, even before he is installed in the job, of a State visit to the UK with all that entails. God alone knows what Trump might tweet about the Queen and Prince Philip. If Air Force One isn't grand enough for him, I fear the faded charms of Buck House and Windsor Castle might get the full treatment from the Tweeter-in-Chief.

Instead of saying "there is no vacancy" as UK ambassador, Mrs May would garner more respect—not least from Trump, given bullies only understand the language of strength—if she politely suggested he get on with sorting out his own team and leave her to decide hers; and put talk of Windsor Castle on the back burner until he shows he understands that for all that he won as a change candidate, there is a purpose to diplomatic protocols and he would be wise to follow at least some of them.

There has been a lot of talk of Trump's Presidency being 'normalised' and of course the good losing of Obama and Clinton helped with that. But both the manner of his win and much of his conduct since have not been normal and there should be far greater resistance to the idea that they are.

In both Trump and Brexit, we have seen victories secured by myth now being followed by fantasy. The myths were helped by the lies they told. The fantasies are that everything is going to be alright. Trump will be like Reagan, say the normalisers. But the evidence suggests he won't. Brexit will go fine. But the evidence suggests it won't. I thought businessman Charles Dunstone put it well this week … "What I feel about Brexit is that it's a little bit like we've jumped off a 100-storey building and have just passed the 50th floor and we're saying, 'Actually this isn't so absolutely terrible' —but we haven't hit the pavement yet."

In fantasyland not only do we have to accept defeat. We seemingly have to accept anything the victors throw at us. We have to let Trump think he can say or do what the hell he likes. We have to believe that anyone who dares suggest there may be a downside to Brexit is deeply unpatriotic, enemies of the people, their views utterly irrelevant.

Several months on from the vote surely there should have been a clearer path laid out to this bright shiny new future we are all being asked to believe lies beyond the triggering of Article 50? For Mrs May to be talking of cliff edges and red white and blue Brexit suggests that our government is no clearer about where we are heading.

But one thing I will say for Trump … he was, in many ways, the most erratic of campaigners. In fact, part of his appeal was you could never guess what he would say or do next. But he always returned to the same messages—making America great again, Crooked Hillary, life is rigged by the elite against you. Even when angry, which seemed to be most of the time, he didn't lose sight of what would motivate the voters he needed to win.

He had a message. In his own unique way, he stuck to it. And those of us who believe he will take the world in the wrong direction, and those who think Brexit in the wrong direction, need to keep to our message too. Politics is not like sport, my other great passion. In football, the game ends, the final whistle goes, there is a settled result. Trump won, but he alone does not shape the future. Brexit won, but the Brextremists alone must not be allowed to dictate what "Brexit means Brexit" *actually* means in terms of the laws and practices under which we are governed.

So never stop fighting for what you believe in. Never stop calling out the lies and the excesses. And never stop reminding David Cameron that his referendum was a very very bad idea, the consequences of which will be with us for a long time, all of which makes *me* very angry that the ambitions and needs of my children's generation have been thwarted by the shortsightedness, the fake nostalgia, the loss of historical perspective of our generation, gleefully exploited by the charlatans who led the campaign and the tax-dodging or foreign media barons who so happily and so loudly banged their drums for them.

Thank you.

Viewpoint 2

I Am Brexit. Hear Me Roar?

Jonathon Gatehouse, Charlie Gillis, and Sally Hayden

In the following viewpoint, Jonathon Gatehouse, Charles Gillis, and Sally Hayden survey scholarship and conduct interviews with the intent to understand whether Brexit's anti-elite, anti-globalization rhetoric might resound across Europe. Certainly, the United Kingdom and the rest of the continent have similar goals when it comes to security and climate policy. But will Brexit encourage other nations to distrust integration? Does Brexit mark a revolution? Or is it just an evolution in Britain's necessary, but never quite cheery, relationship with Europe? Gatehouse, Gillis, and Hayden write for the Canadian national affairs magazine Maclean's.

The promised Elvis impersonator never showed up, but the bar was free and the mood triumphant. Up on the 29th floor of London's Millbank Tower, overlooking the Thames and the Houses of Parliament, they wore party hats and Union Jack wristbands, and toasted Britain's decision to leave the European Union with sparkling wine from Italy. The evening, hosted by the Leave.EU campaign, had started as a wake. Faced with an avalanche of last-minute opinion surveys predicting a comfortable victory for the Remain side, both the Conservatives' Boris Johnson and Nigel Farage, the leader of the UK Independence Party, expressed their pessimism and regret as the polls closed. But as the count dragged on into the early hours of the next morning, the number of votes

"Is Brexit the start of a new war against globalization?" by Jonathon Gatehouse, Charlie Gillis and Sally Hayden, Rogers Media, June 25, 2016. Reprinted by Permission.

for Leave slowly caught up to the Remain total, and then began to pull away. Shortly after 4 a.m., with Britain's TV networks having declared the previously unthinkable Brexit an electoral reality, a broadly smiling Farage appeared before a jostling mob of press and a crowd of drunk and ecstatic supporters.

"After 25 years of fighting... we didn't dare to believe it would happen but the people have spoken," he said. "We have fought against the multinationals, we fought against the big merchant banks, we fought against big politics, we fought against lies, corruption and deceit. And we will have done it without having to fight, without a single bullet being fired."

Coming a week after the fatal shooting of Jo Cox, the Labour MP and Remain supporter, his victory speech managed to be both inaccurate and insensitive. (Farage apologized a few hours later.) But the UKIP leader wasn't alone in gloating about the largely peaceful revolution. In the largest electoral turnout since 1992, 16 million Britons opted to stay in the EU, and 17 million voted to get out: a close 52 to 48 per cent split that appears to be sufficient to trigger a slow and painful divorce from Europe, and sent political and economic shock waves around the globe.

By the time dawn broke, the British pound was trading at a 31-year low. And before most people had their second cup of coffee, David Cameron announced his intention to step down as prime minister and let someone else deal with the fallout from his failed and faulty Remain campaign.

For months, Britons were told that leaving the EU would be a mistake of historic proportions. A made-in-the-U.K. recession and massive job losses were only some of the nightmare scenarios conjured by the likes of Britain's chancellor, the governor of the Bank of England, the head of the International Monetary Fund, U.S. President Barack Obama, European leaders, OECD economists and every cultural figure from Jude Law to Stephen Hawking. But "Project Fear," as it was dubbed, lost out to a Leave campaign that focused on an entirely different set of terrors. Preaching a pressing need to limit immigration and protect the borders against migrants, in order to preserve both the U.K.'s culture and way of life, Leave proponents found a large and receptive audience. Even though their claim that the EU "costs" Britain $620 million a week was widely discredited, many voters warmed to the promise of bringing both control and money "back home" and reinvesting in spheres like education and the National Health Service.

The world's fifth-largest economy turning its back on the globe's largest trading block is momentous news regardless of the motivation. Many fear it may prove to be the destabilizing domino that knocks other, less robust, nations like Greece, Italy and Spain from the European Union. Could the backlash against the Continent play into a wider war on globalization?

Britain's decision to rebuild its borders seemed to resonate around the world with leaders of various political stripes. Touching down in Scotland the morning after the vote for a business visit to one of his golf resorts, Donald Trump hailed Leave's "great victory" over the "rule of the global elite." Linking it to his own crusade to ban Muslims' entry into the U.S., build border walls and tear up trade deals, the billionaire and presumptive Republican nominee for president predicted the rise of a mass movement. "People want to take their country back. They want to have independence in a sense," he said. "You see it all over Europe and many other cases where they want to take their borders back. They want to take their monetary [sic] back. They want to take a lot of things back... I think you are going to have this more and more."

He was not alone. Vladimir Putin spoke approvingly of Brexit too, calling it "understandable" that the British were concerned about security amidst Europe's migrant crisis, and tired of paying for other people. "No one wants to feed and subsidize poorer economies, to support other states, support entire nations," said the Russian president. Marie Le Pen, the leader of France's far-right National Front Party tweeted her congratulations to the Leave campaign, making it clear she found inspiration in the result. "Victory for freedom!" Le Pen wrote. "As I've said for years, we need the same referendum in France and in the EU countries."

From the opposite end of the political spectrum, Bernie Sanders applauded too. Appearing on MSNBC, the U.S. senator and socialist lamented the breakdown in international co-operation, but suggested the system made it inevitable. "What this vote is about is an indication that the global economy is not working for everybody," he said. "It's not working in the United States for everybody and it's not working in the U.K. for everybody."

One doesn't have to scratch much below the surface of the referendum results to discover that the decisive ballots were cast by those who haven't shared in EU's vaunted benefits—namely older voters who live outside of Britain's major cities. Of the 30 voting districts with the most residents aged 65 and over, only two voted Remain. The split was even starker when it came to education, with 66 per cent of those who left school at age 16 voting to leave, while 71 per cent of those with university degrees opting to stay.

The numbers square with pre-referendum polls that suggested 73 per cent of voters aged 18–29 wanted to remain part of the EU, while 63 per cent over 60 wanted to get out. It all goes a long way to explaining why young protesters gathered outside 10 Downing Street the morning after the vote, bearing placards with slogans like "Don't f–k with our future."

The Leave vote was also decidedly English. Remain carried the day in Scotland and Northern Ireland, raising questions as to whether the United Kingdom will survive the wrenching process of withdrawal. Cameron won his first referendum gamble, the 2014 vote on Scottish independence. But that campaign made much of the advantages conferred by Britain's membership in the EU and now looks a bit shortsighted. Nicola Sturgeon, Scotland's first minister and a proponent of Scottish independence, was quick off the mark following the Leave vote, noting that six out of every 10 Scots had opted for Remain. "We voted to renew our reputation as an outward-looking, open and inclusive country," she said in a statement. "It remains my passionate belief that it is better for all parts of the U.K. to be members of the European Union." A second referendum on a Scottish breakaway is now "highly likely,"

Sturgeon added. Martin McGuinness, the deputy first minister of Northern Ireland, and a member of Sinn Féin, raised similar concerns and called for a vote to unite the Emerald Isle.

Whatever the deciding demographic, there's little question that Britain's gesture will sound alarm bells throughout the industrialized world. Last winter, Cameron used the threat of the impending referendum to negotiate a sweetheart deal with the EU, winning concessions on limiting migrants' access to government benefits, and a guarantee the U.K. wouldn't have to participate in future euro bailouts. But Britons still voted to flee a union that has been held up as a model of global economic integration, peace and prosperity. And in this case, who is pulling the plug matters every bit as much as why.

The U.K., a country of 65 million, punches far above its weight in international organizations like the G7, NATO and the United Nations. It is home to one of the world's most educated populations and, in London, one of its most important financial centres—the key entry point for investment capital flowing into Europe. If a country like that sees no promise in a borderless, global economy, what nation possibly could?

The out vote is a stinging repudiation of ideas Western governments have pushed for decades: that economic globalization was a tide to lift all boats; that integration is good; that advanced economies will be the big winners of the globalized market, shedding smoke-belching industries in favour of specialized work based on skill and knowledge.

In some ways, argues Martin Ruhs, an associate professor of political economy at Oxford University, the U.K. has become a victim of its own success. Protected by its refusal to join the eurozone, the country's economy has prospered while others in the zone have struggled to prop up Greece, Spain and the other weaklings, becoming a magnet for those seeking work. And the EU, which demands unfettered movement, hasn't been quite so rigorous about standardizing wages or tackling laws and collective agreements that make it harder to hire and fire on the Continent.

"The U.K. has both the most flexible labour market and the highest demand for low-wage workers," says Ruhs, who studies the effects of migration within the EU. "The EU really hasn't done a good job and recognizing those structural differences."

Ruhs says there is really no hard data to back up the Leave side's claims about a flood of arrivals from the Continent putting pressure on schools, housing and hospitals. But that really doesn't matter since most Britons believe that it's true. "The idea that it's out of control and can't be managed within the EU is what became so powerful," he says. "At the end of the day, those concerns about immigration trumped the economic fears."

John Helliwell, a professor emeritus of economics at the University of British Columbia, believes the referendum result will cause political leaders to reconsider the common assumption that greater integration is always better. Globalization is not going away, he says, but the preferable model for most countries may let them "keep the essential tools they need to manage their own societies in the interest of their citizens, while giving them friendly and co-operative contacts with the rest of the world." In the case of the EU, a more workable solution might have been to give national governments greater control over the admission of EU-country passport holders and strike a balance between labour market needs and pressures on social welfare systems.

It might also help for proponents of globalism to stop overselling its benefits, and trying to engineer society to accommodate it, says Helliwell. "Most of economic and social life is lived pretty locally," notes the professor, who explored these pitfalls in his 2002 book *Globalization and Well-being*. "You don't need to align many of your institutions with those in other countries to get the main advantages from it. The world trade system has been a pretty open one for the last 50 years."

European cohesion has been under increasing threat in recent years. A report released this spring by the European Council on Foreign Relations found that the refugee and migrant crisis has exposed "deeply rooted divisions" and created "new political cleavages between member states." (On June 23, the day of the vote, 40 vessels carrying 4,500 more migrants made their made across the Mediterranean from Libya, bringing the total number of overall arrivals by sea in 2016 to 215,000.) Denmark, Germany, Sweden and Austria have all reinstituted forms of border control, contravening the terms of the Schengen agreement and "ring fencing" to defend their national status quo. "Political populists all over Europe have sensed this change," warned the think tank. And "as diverse as they otherwise may be, the new populist nationalists in Europe have one common view: that the pooling of sovereignty is a key problem."

Amy Verdun, a University of Victoria political scientist who specializes in globalization and European integration, calls it a worrying trend. "If those groups become stronger, they could start asking to have [their own] referendums to vote their way out," she says. "There might be a ripple effect because of this mass psychology."

Europe's nativist political parties have already found fodder in the steady flow of bad news out of Brussels over the past few years. The Greek crisis, with its attendant fears over the financial stability of Spain and Portugal, forced the EU to expand and deepen, notes Verdun, setting up new institutions to backstop and supervise the banking sector. Then came the refugee crisis, stoking fears over national identity and the stress on the social safety nets in countries like the Netherlands and Germany. Together, says Verdun, these events have overshadowed the benefits that average Europeans have gained through membership, which seem abstract next to the hard sums that rich EU countries pour into the organization each year.

Britain's impending divorce from the union—a untried process that promises to be fraught and lengthy—might well make matter worse. Jan Techau, the director of Carnegie Europe, a Brussels-based think tank, says the EU is in crisis mode. "Overall, the sense is 'Oh my God, what have we gotten ourselves into.' " Already, it's clear that there will be two distinct camps with the union when it comes to the pending negotiations. One led by the presidents of the European Council and Commission, Donald Tusk and Jean-Claude Juncker, will push for a quick break and terms that are as difficult as possible for the U.K. when it comes to its future access to the Common Market. "They want to set a precedent, a very painful precedent, so that this entire thing looks like a very unattractive model," says Techau. And while the other camp, led by the Irish, Dutch and Austrians, favours a much longer divorce process, their plan is pretty much the same: to maximize the economic pain for U.K. residents—albeit with a different end goal, showing British voters the error of their ways and forcing the next prime minister into some sort of revised, but continuing relationship.

Techau believes the EU will survive either way—few, if any, of its remaining members have the both the desire to leave and the leverage to extract themselves, he says. In many ways, he argues, the union remains a success story. "We tend to look at the horrible news, but in reality large parts of the EU are quite functional and producing public good for the member states that they don't won't to lose out on," he says. "This doesn't have to be existential at all."

Reality also dictates that the U.K. will want to continue to pursue some common policies and goals with the EU, in areas like security and the fight against climate change. (Britain signed on to the bloc's carbon-trading market as well as the 2020 emission reduction targets and last year's Paris deal.)

The question then becomes whether Brexit is a revolution, or rather an evolution.

Britons will have plenty of time to contemplate the riddle. Estimates of just how long it will take to fully extract themselves from a 43-year marriage with Europe are generally in the seven- to 10-year range, making it an issue that will dog at least two more governments.

On the night of the referendum, there was a decent crowd at the Drum Wetherspon, a pub in the east London neighbourhood of Leyton. Part of a national chain owned by pro-Brexit multi-millionaire Tim Martin, who had ordered the distribution of half a million beer mats printed with his arguments for voting Leave. "He's allowed to do what he likes, I suppose, it's his business," said David Tomlinson, resting his glass of Tuborg on Martin's reasoning. The 60-year-old was on a visit from Liverpool, where he owns a business that manages multi-storey carparks. A trim man with a glinting, gold neck chain, he spoke animatedly about his distrust of politics and ineffective politicians. He said his business has benefited from Britain's membership in the EU. A remain backer, the EU referendum marked the first time he had ever voted.

On Thursday nights, Wetherspoon sells itself as the "nation's biggest curry house," serving up chicken korma, lamb rogan josh, and chicken balti for less than $14, pint included. The famously cheap alcohol fuelled lots of chatter about politics. In the smoking area out the back, a 35-year-old named Lubo from Slovakia was leaning against a pillar while thoughtfully puffing on a cigarette. He said he came to Britain in 2005, "right away when they opened the borders. I wanted to change my life." His friend Mark, a 48-year-old who also works in IT and has always lived in Leyton, debated with Lubo about what impact a Brexit would have for EU citizens in the U.K. before leaning forward to quietly admit: "If I was to be honest with you I'd say most people here don't understand [what's at stake in the referendum], I'd say most professionals don't either."

Neither, it might be said, do the elite.

Over at the Leave.EU party, Piers Corbyn—older brother of Labour Leader Jeremy—was excited when the final result came in for Birmingham, showing an unexpected Brexit vote. "[It's] historic for the U.K. which means we're now in control of our own lawmaking and our own borders... That is going to be better, and the key thing is the democracy," he said. His younger brother now faces a non-confidence motion from dissenting members of his own party, upset at his lacklustre performance on behalf of Remain.

Piers, who was involved in the Leave.EU campaign from the beginning, maintained that his brother was still the best man for the Labour job, because he has been "quite rational" about the downsides of supporting Brussels.

Brexit is the EU's Funeral, Says Marine Le Pen

The president of the National Front, a right-wing Eurosceptic party, issued the warning to Jean-Claude Juncker, the president of the European Commission after branding his state of the Union speech to MEPs at the European Parliament in Strasbourg, France, "insipid."

[…]

She said: "Well Mr Juncker, quite rarely have we seen such an insipid and faulty speech.

"This is basically almost like a funeral for the European Union, but perhaps we should admit there was a very good point on humour where you said you were the hero of combatting fiscal optimisation for multinationals.

"But really, you haven't been paying attention to the ambition of people in the European Union to reestablish and retake their sovereignty and their independence.

"Brexit has really broken a taboo. The Brits have shown us that you can leave the European Union and you can come out better.

"The catastrophic visions were just a lie. The UK is doing quite well, the shock that you wanted to see has now turned into trust, everybody thought there was going to be apocalypse falling on the UK but that didn't happen.

You've shown a disdain for the referendum, so what are you protecting us from? Freedom? Democracy?

"It is time to move on and I think that people need a project for the future. Let's be democrats, finally, and let the people decide."

[…]

"Over the past four years, I have said that I will be organising a referendum so French people can express themselves on the issue of France leaving the European Union."

– "'This is a funeral' Le Pen predicts the end of the EU as she promises FREXIT referendum," by Joe Barnes, Express Newspapers Ltd., September 15, 2016.

As the victory party finally rolled up, Linda Stanbury sat on a bench outside the office tower, watching the sun rise. The 54-year-old, who runs a counselling and well-being business and lives in south London, said it was one of the greatest days of her life. "I feel elated, this is the happiest day since the Berlin Wall came down. This is the people speaking, and it's fantastic," she said. "We won't be strangled by the noose around our necks of the European happy club . . . I've seen this country slip-sliding away."

Britons have voted for change. Just how big a one, we'll find out.

Viewpoint 3

In Brexit, There Are No Winners

Wolfgang Münchau

In the following viewpoint, writer Wolfgang Münchau observes that an agreement struck between the UK and the EU a few months before the June 23, 2016, referendum vote may have sown the seeds for Brexit by creating a "formal exemption from the goal of an ever-closer union." Münchau, who is an associate editor of the Financial Times, *warns that, "if you divide a union you end up with disunion. You cannot have it both ways.*

One of the few certain statements one can make about Friday's agreement between European leaders and David Cameron is that it will have little impact on the June 23 referendum on British membership of the EU. It is far too technical to sway many voters.

Even those who have made an effort to understand its nuances cannot be sure of exactly how much would unravel in the legislative and judicial processes that will follow. It is, after all, the first such agreement of its kind.

My pro-European friends in Britain tend to look at it in a pragmatic way. It was good enough for the British prime minister to launch the referendum with a recommendation that the UK should remain an EU member. It did the job.

From the perspective of the rest of the EU, the deal is awkward. EU leaders calculated, rightly in my view, that the cost of Brexit —a British exit from the EU—would be too high at a time when

---

"Concessions to Britain will create a two-tier Europe," by Wolfgang Münchau, The Financial Times Ltd, February 21, 2016.

the future of the EU itself is in doubt. They were ready to pay ransom money to prevent a calamity. The question is: did they pay too much?

Their single most important concession is their agreement, for the first time, to a two-tier Europe. This is not an opt-out, an exemption or a derogation. This is not a Europe of variable speeds or variable geometry—expressions that have been used in the past to denote different degrees of integration. This is a formal exemption from the goal of ever-closer union. I am not sure whether this has any legal significance but it matters as a political statement.

How can the EU pursue ever-closer union when one of its most important EU members enjoys a permanent exemption? Core-Europe projects—those pursued by only a subset of members—cannot be the answer. They did not work well in the past. The EU has a legal mechanism in place that would allow a minimum of nine countries to seek deeper integration among each other. If you divide a union you end up with disunion. You cannot have it both ways.

The latest such project is the financial transactions tax. It started out with 11 member states. Then Estonia dropped out. And now Belgium has doubts. It is theoretically still possible for the remaining nine countries to go ahead but some doubt whether they should do this. The fewer countries that participate, the greater the chances that this tax might simply drive their banks into EU countries without such a tax.

This agreement adds to economic policy fragmentation. It recognises that eurozone and non-eurozone countries might have different needs to secure financial stability. Much of the debate in the European Council has been whether Britain should have its own rule book: ground rules for the financial sector such as capital rules and procedures for bank resolution. In the end, the EU managed to keep up the appearance of a single EU-wide rule book with some special provisions for Britain.

But how could different regulatory regimes for the financial sector work for a monetary union whose main financial centre—London—is geographically outside its own borders? According to this text, the European Central Bank and other institutions involved in financial regulation should apply supervisory decisions "in a more uniform manner than corresponding rules to be applied by national authorities of member states that do not take part in the banking union".

This is probably the most hilarious euphemism of the text. European banks are in a bad state. The banking union was supposed to be the answer, but is incomplete because it lacks a fiscal support and joint deposit insurance.

Britain is not part of it but it is part of the EU's single market for financial services. This exemption is hard to justify.

What about the social benefits, the big political issue in the UK? The provision that allows the UK government to restrict in-work benefits for non-British EU employees for a period of up to four years will make it marginally harder for some to move across borders.

This is not going to be the end of free movement of labour. But one would have thought that if the EU really took the concept of an ever-closer union seriously, policy should encourage cross-border labour movements, not do the opposite. Other countries will no doubt ask for—and get—similar exemptions.

There is a risk that following a vote to remain in the EU, the deal may not be implemented in full, prompting conspiracy theories about how the EU deliberately misled the British electorate.

If the deal is implemented in full, it will end the idea of ever-closer union. And if the British vote to leave, the deal will become null and void. Britain would enter a long process negotiating its exit from the EU. I struggle to see any good outcomes.

Viewpoint 4

Will Brexit Prompt Scottish Independence? Not So Fast

John Curtice

After Brexit, some were convinced that Scotland would try again to secure independence from the United Kingdom, since nearly two-thirds of Scottish voters wanted the UK to remain in the EU. A 2017 survey, however, puts that line of thinking into question. John Curtice, a professor of politics at Strathclyde University, notes in this viewpoint that Brexit has not strengthened Scotland's independence movement. Fifty-four percent still believe it's best for Scotland to remain part of the UK; just 41 percent think "Scotland's economy will be weaker as a result of leaving the EU," and only a handful of voters worry that Brexit will undermine Scotland's control of its own laws.

The last fortnight has seemingly seen Nicola Sturgeon's options narrow significantly. The Prime Minister has set out a vision of Brexit that is the very opposite of the Scottish Government's stated preference to stay in the single market and continue to accept freedom of movement. The Supreme Court has ruled that the UK government is not legally obliged to seek Holyrood's consent before giving the EU notice that the UK wishes to leave. Meanwhile the Scottish Secretary, David Mundell, has poured a lot of cold water on the idea that post-Brexit Scotland might be able to have a more liberal policy than the rest of the UK in respect of migrants from the EU.

"Ms. Sturgeon's Brexit Difficulties," by John Curtice, What Scotland Thinks, January 29, 2017. Reprinted by Permission.

Between them these developments would—as the First Minister herself has acknowledged—seem to leave her with little option but to hold a second independence referendum if Scotland is to maintain the close relationship with the EU that she believes is essential for Scotland's future prosperity.

However, a new poll from Panelbase published in today's Sunday Times adds to the existing doubts about whether seeking a Yes vote in a second referendum vote on the back of the argument that independence is the only way Scotland can continue to enjoy a close relationship with the rest of the EU will prove an effective strategy.

Not that Scotland has gone off the idea of staying in the EU. Today's poll suggests that 61% would now vote to remain in the EU, a figure that is not significantly different from the 62% that were found to have voted for Remain when the ballot boxes were opened north of the border in June last year. However, today's poll also affirms previous poll findings that, despite the SNP's advocacy of"'independence in Europe," Brexit significantly divides the nationalist movement. As many as 35% of those who say they voted Yes to independence in September 2014 state they would vote to leave if a second EU referendum were held now. The willingness of this group to vote for independence is hardly likely to be bolstered by any pro-independence campaign that focused on keeping Scotland in the EU.

What we do learn anew from today's poll is that support for the Scottish Government's policy towards Scotland's future relationship with the EU is not as widespread as it might like. True, there is little dissent from the idea that Scotland should continue to trade freely with the EU. As many as 65% agree with the proposition that "Companies in other EU countries should be allowed to sell goods as easily in Scotland as they can in their own country," while just 11% disagree. Such figures suggest most people in Scotland would be quite happy for their country to remain a member of the single market.

However, only 40% agree that "People from other European countries should still have an automatic right to come to Scotland to live and work should they so wish" while almost as many, 36%, disagree. Meanwhile, amongst those who voted No to independence in September 2014 (some of whom the SNP need to win over if it is to win a second independence referendum) only 28% agree with the proposition while 46% disagree. Public opinion in Scotland may be more liberal on immigration than it is in England, but linking independence to retaining freedom of movement is not obviously going to prove an effective way of increasing support for independence.

At the same time, it would seem that a majority of people in Scotland are not convinced that Brexit will prove as deleterious as the Scottish Government suggests. Just 40% think that immigration to Scotland from outside the UK will actually fall as a result of leaving the EU. But more importantly, perhaps, only 41% think that Scotland's economy will be weaker as a result of leaving the EU. While this figure may be nearly double the proportion (21%) who think the economy would be stronger, it still represents well under half of all voters. Here it should be borne in mind that one of the key reasons why the Remain camp lost the EU referendum across the UK is that only around two in five voters believed that the UK economy would actually suffer from Brexit—the rest simply reckoned (or hoped) it would not make much difference and largely went on to vote for Leave. In any event, one might imagine that Nicola Sturgeon should not need any lessons in the potential limitations of arguments that look like "Project Fear."

Equally, there is little sign that voters share the concern of some in the SNP that the UK government will use Brexit as an opportunity to take back some of the powers and responsibilities that the Scottish Parliament currently enjoys. Only 15% think that Scotland will have less control over its laws as a result of Brexit. Most (48%) simply think it will not make much difference.

All in all, then, it is perhaps not surprising that today's poll finds that there is still a small but clear majority in favour of Scotland staying in the UK. After leaving aside those who said, "Don't Know," Panelbase put support for Yes at 46%, with No at 54%. That actually represents a one point drop in support for independence as compared with the company's last poll last September. Such a drop could arise simply as a result of the chance variation to which all polls are subject, but the figures are in accord with the findings of polls undertaken by YouGov and BMG before Christmas that also suggested that support for independence is now at more or less the same level as it was in the September 2014 referendum.

Some voters have changed their mind in the wake of the EU referendum. But, as we have pointed out before, the problem from the SNP's point of view is that for every voter who has switched from No to Yes following the UK-wide decision to leave the EU, another has switched from Yes to No. YouGov demonstrated this quite clearly in an analysis published on Friday. Thus, while only 74% of those who voted No in 2014 and Remain in 2016 would vote the same way again in an independence referendum, equally only 65% of those Yes voters who backed Leave say they would back independence again. In contrast, and as we might anticipate, No voters who voted to Leave are still nearly all happy to stay in the UK (93% would again vote No), while Yes voters who voted to Remain are also still largely loyal to the independence cause (86% would vote the same way).

Meanwhile, it would seem that supporters of independence themselves may also be coming to the conclusion that Brexit may not provide an opportune moment for a second independence referendum after all. Just 27% of all voters now think that an independence referendum should be held before the UK leaves the EU. That represents a drop of five points since last September and one of no less than 16 points compared with the position immediately after the EU referendum result became known. Even amongst those who voted Yes in September 2014 rather less than half (47%) now think a second independence referendum should be held before the UK leaves the EU.

Still, perhaps for Ms Sturgeon there is a silver lining to this particular cloud. If many of her supporters are not convinced that an early indyref2 should be held in order to avoid Brexit, perhaps this means it will be easier for her to take a second referendum "off the table" should she decide that holding such a ballot looks too risky after all.

Viewpoint 5

The Brexit White Paper Has Lots of White Space

Maria Garcia

On February 1, 2017, the House of Commons voted to give Prime Minister Theresa May the power to trigger Article 50, the provision in the Treaty of Lisbon that empowers any member to withdraw from the European Union. The following day, David Davis, secretary of state for exiting the European Union, presented an outline of the UK's proposed exit strategy. In the following viewpoint, Maria Garcia, senior lecturer in international relations at the University of Bath, finds flaws—or rather ambiguities—in that document, particularly in its language around trade. Moreover, she is of the opinion that the white paper "underestimates the challenges of negotiating trade deals," and, as such, the UK may find favorable provisions hard to come by.

Two of the 12 priorities set out in the UK government's Brexit white paper are focused on trade:

- Ensuring free trade with European markets
- Securing new trade agreements with countries outside the EU

In terms of trade with the EU—the UK's largest trading partner—the white paper makes clear that the UK will not be seeking membership of the single market and the customs union. Instead it will pursue "an ambitious and comprehensive Free Trade Agreement and a new customs agreement." This is in line with the

---

"What the Brexit white paper says (and doesn't say) about trade," by Maria Garcia, The Conversation, 02/03/2017. https://theconversation.com/what-the-brexit-white-paper-says-and-doesnt-say-about-trade-72384.

government's desire not to abide by the single market's freedom of movement rules.

However, the white paper still lacks clarity on the matter. It stresses the interconnection of the UK and EU markets in many sectors (automobiles, agriculture, transport, financial and other services), and argues for the need to reach an agreement that guarantees continued stability in the trade relationship. Yet, by leaving the single market and customs union, the conditions of trade will be different. In its desire for continuity in the parts that are seen as beneficial to the government, while relinquishing participation in less desirable areas, the document bears some echoes of the "have our cake and eat it" approach.

A preferential trade agreement with the EU, by its nature, cannot be as inclusive as full membership of the single market. This is recognised in the white paper with the reiteration of a bespoke deal that differs from any other formal relationship the EU has established with non-EU members. The European partners have made it clear that a bespoke future agreement for the UK cannot give all the trade benefits of single market access minus the movement of people and European Court of Justice jurisdiction. So the exact nature of the proposed Brexit deal remains unclear.

Moreover, the white paper emphasises close ties in all sectors, without indicating government priorities. The challenge of specifying which sectors they will seek to defend most in negotiations, and which they are willing to sacrifice, remains.

The white paper states there may be European programmes that the UK wishes to participate in and, in exchange for that, the government will pay into the EU budget. There is no indication what these programmes may be, but are likely to be education and scientific research programmes. This should not be particularly controversial as many non-EU countries participate in a number of EU programmes, such as Israel. Likewise, given that the UK already applies EU customs procedures, a customs agreement should, in principle, be relatively simple to reach.

Rest of The World

Securing trade agreements with other states, like the US or Asian economies, will also create winners and losers within the UK. Trump's desire to defend US manufacturing and Asian competitiveness in this sector could make it challenging for UK negotiators to get winning deals for automobiles and other manufacturers. Meanwhile, improving market access for UK service providers abroad—a long-standing goal of UK and EU trade policy—will also encounter resistance, especially in Asia, where states like India attempt to link access to its market to developed states by accepting short-term Indian migrants to deliver services. The government's enthusiasm for these deals fails to take this into account.

Officially, the UK cannot legally sign trade deals with other states until leaving the EU fully. Crucially, until the government is entirely clear on what its post-Brexit tariff quotas will be and, more broadly, which sectors it wants to prioritise in gaining access to overseas markets (as well as those it may be willing to sacrifice) substantive negotiations cannot be undertaken.

The white paper underestimates the challenges of negotiating trade deals. While other states, including the US, may well have the political will and desire to negotiate post-Brexit deals with the UK, they will seek to defend their own interests in those agreements. President Trump's "America first" approach makes that clear. But even other partners like Australia and New Zealand will seek their own gains. They will demand more access for their agricultural products, for example, possibly to the detriment of UK agricultural producers, who will have also lost EU agricultural support.

Negotiating trade deals is a tremendous task and requires clarity for each and every economic sector involved. Unfortunately, the white paper gives little detail on this. Considering the UK is leaving the world's largest trading bloc—which brings with it a huge amount of clout in negotiations—it will need to sort out these details for its forthcoming negotiations.

Theresa May's 12-point Brexit plan

- Provide certainty about the process of leaving the EU
- Control of our own laws
- Strengthen the Union between the four nations of the United Kingdom
- Maintain the Common Travel Area with Ireland
- Brexit must mean control of the number of people who come to Britain from Europe
- Rights for EU nationals in Britain and British nationals in the EU
- Protect workers' rights
- Free trade with European markets through a free trade agreement
- New trade agreements with other countries
- The best place for science and innovation
- Co-operation in the fight against crime and terrorism
- A smooth, orderly Brexit

Theresa May's Brexit speech: Key points

- A final deal on Britain's exit from the EU will be put to a vote of both Houses of Parliament
- Ireland will have a common travel area between UK and Irish republic, "which will protect the security of UK"
- May wants to guarantee the rights of EU nationals in Britain, and Britons living in Europe, as soon as possible.
- Britain will leave the single market. The Government will seek "the greatest possible access with a fully-reciprocal free trade deal." May indicated that Britain could pay if necessary, but would stop making the contributions it makes now.
- May wants to see "a phased process of implementation of new arrangements outside the E" from 2019
- Theresa May prefers "no deal" than a "bad deal" telling EU leaders punishing Britain would be "an act of calamitous self-harm"

— "Theresa May's Brexit speech in full," by Theresa May, Telegraph Media Group, January 17, 2017.

VIEWPOINT 6

You Say Democracy, I Say Democracy

Andrew Hines

The breach between Leavers and Remainers has rendered the meaning of democracy sharply uncertain. So writes Andrew Hines, a PhD student at the University of London, in the following viewpoint. For Leavers, Brexit was democracy at its finest, an enactment of public desire. But for Remainers, who tend to think in a democracy representatives restrain and refine the wild will of the populace, it was a catastrophic miscarriage. There were, in effect, two referenda on June 23: One on the UK's continued membership in the EU and another on the meaning of the word "democracy" itself.

Ever since the EU referendum, an increasingly poisonous debate has raged about "the will of the people" and how it should be delivered. Both Remainers and Brexiteers are scratching their heads at what is clearly a clash of two different ideals of democracy. The clash is partly linguistic. On both sides of the Brexit debate, you hear phrases like "will of the people" and "democratic representation". But each side seems to be describing a different kind of democracy. The gap between word and meaning is causing a rift in the democratic process itself.

One of the key philosophical and scientific discoveries of the modern era was that the language we use to talk about abstract concepts shapes how we understand those concepts. The word "democracy" is no exception. In 1835, Alexis de Tocqueville

---

"After Brexit, what does democracy mean?" by Andrew Hines, The Conversation, 11/24/2016. https://theconversation.com/after-brexit-what-does-democracy-mean-69251.

compared it to the growth of a person when he likened the American democractic process to the growth from infancy to adulthood.

The metaphor of democracy as a powerful body extends back to ancient Greece. *Demos* means the people or the multitudes. And in Greek mythology, Kratos, one of Zeus' enforcers, is the personification of power and authority. So, when the *Demos* have *Kratia*, you have an authoritative or powerful multitude.

Since June 23, it has become clear that the definition of the language of democracy that is thrown around in the British media reveals significant ideological clashes.

Day after day, pro-Brexit commentators and publications have stood behind phrases like "will of the people" when talking about democracy.

Gina Miller, the businesswoman who took a case to the high court to argue that the government couldn't go ahead with Brexit without first consulting parliament, was labelled a "traitor to democracy" for her actions. Yet she stated that she led the action against the government precisely because of her concern that democracy was under threat.

After one anti-Brexit march, meanwhile, protesting remainers were accused of attempting to "thwart the people's will" and "crush public opinion."

In this view, democracy means a path towards a particular goal that the people collectively want. Will is obviously our ability to choose one thing out of many things such as the choice to vote leave instead of remain. The French philosopher Jean-Jacques Rousseau applied this to politics during the French Revolution when he stated that the law was meant to "express the general will."

Representation

But the other side of the debate sees itself as equally concerned about the need to honour democracy. The Brexit-sceptical Guardian urged despairing Remainers not to resort to "undemocratic moves" —such as urging parliament to ignore the vote—to achieve their goal of staying in the EU.

However, it has also outlined the legal ways in which "the will of the people" could be legitimately and democratically overturned such as by a vote by MP's against triggering article 50 or holding a second referendum if evidence suggests that a large number of those who voted leave have changed their mind.

This is the other view of democracy that seems to clash with the "will of the people." It is one that describes democratic representation rather than general will as outlined by Rousseau.

Many people—particularly Remainers—think it undemocratic for the government to plough on with Brexit without a debate about it in parliament. This is of course the line that Miller picked up on when defending herself against people who called her actions undemocratic. Miller said:

> *All the people who have been saying "we need to take back control," "we need sovereignty," well you can't have it with one hand and then with the other say, "I'm going to bypass it now and not seek consultation from the representatives in parliament."*

Miller is making a quite literal appeal to democratic representation in parliament. But she is also referring to the ideal of the democratic process itself. Walter Bagehot, who wrote the famous 1867 work English Constitution, said that representative democracy is "government by discussion." And in the UK, the vehicle for that discussion is parliament. So, while the word "representation" does not refer to the particular goal of the people's collective will, it does refer to the goal of democracy itself.

This is an ideal of democracy framed by the representation of the public by elected officials. In the context of the Brexit debate, that means the people have given their view on the general direction of travel the country should take but their elected representatives should fill in the detail.

As we decide how Brexit is to be delivered, we need to decide what the word "democracy" means in modern Britain. After the referendum, is the will of the people being thwarted by parliamentary discussion or is it best represented by it?

This linguistic crisis of the meaning of democracy is far from a quibble about semantics. These two words—will and representation—frame two different ideals of one of the West's most cherished ideas. Now the discord about which word best represents British democracy is threatening to tear the practical process of that very idea apart.

Chronology

1957

March 25 Six nations—Belgium, France, Italy, Luxembourg, the Netherlands, and West Germany—form the European Economic Community (EEC) to strengthen trade ties and foster import/export fluidity.

1973

January 1 The United Kingdom joins the European Economic Community, a move that Prime Minister Edward Heath says "will enable us to be more efficient and more competitive in gaining more markets not only in Europe but in the rest of the world."

1984

June 25–26 Prime Minister Margaret Thatcher travels to Fontainebleau, France, where she meets with the European Council and secures what is now known as the UK Rebate. Going forward, 66 percent of the UK's financial contributions to the EU's annual budget will be returned.

1992

February 7 Members of the European Community sign the Treaty of European Union (a.k.a., the Maastricht Treaty), which formally establishes the EU and calls for the establishment of a continental currency.

1993

September 3 Members of the Anti-Federalist League found a new political organization: The UK Independence Party (UKIP). The primary goal is get the UK out of the EU, and, from the outset, the party opposes immigration and espouses libertarian fiscal policies.

1999

January 1 Every EU nation except the UK and Denmark adopts the euro as their currency.

2004

October 29 During the national elections, the Liberal Democrats, Labour, and Conservative parties all say they want to hold a referendum on ratification of the new EU Constitution; however, the constitution is soon defeated by referenda in France and the Netherlands.

2013

January 22 Prime Minister David Cameron announces that if his party, the Conservatives, is successful in the coming election, he will schedule a referendum vote in 2017 so that British citizens can decide once and for all whether they wish to remain in the European Union.

2015

May 27 Parliament passes the European Union Referendum Bill, which authorizes the referendum vote. Meanwhile, Cameron begins conversations with European heads of state aimed at giving the UK a more favorable relationship with the EU without pulling out altogether.

2016

February 19 Cameron convinces the EU member states to agree to a set of adaptations to the UK's EU membership. It includes an "emergency brake" that allows the UK to limit in-work benefits for people from other EU nations. It also frees the UK from the EU's "ever closer union" clause.

February 20 Cameron schedules the referendum for June 23, 2016.

February 21 London's Mayor Boris Johnson announces that he will campaign for the UK's exit from the EU. He joins Justice Secretary Michael Gove, giving the leave movement a powerful face. The Leave EU campaign uses propaganda to convince voters that millions of immigrants will flock to the UK if the nation remains part of the EU.

April 22 President Barack Obama, on a visit to London, warns leaving the EU may harm the UK's trade relationship with the United States. "I think it's fair to say that maybe at some point down the line there might be a UK–US trade agreement, but it's not going to happen any time soon because our focus is in negotiating with a big bloc, the European Union, to get a trade agreement done," he says. "The UK is going to be in the back of the queue."

June 1 Presidential candidate Donald Trump is asked by a reporter for his position on Brexit. Trump replies, "Huh?"

June 15 Chancellor of the exchequer George Osborne releases a mock budget to demonstrate what Brexit could bring about in terms of national finances. It calls for £30 billion in tax hikes and spending cuts.

June 16 Jo Cox, a member of Parliament and staunch supporter of the European Union, is murdered by Thomas Mair, a neo-Nazi.

June 23 Referendum day. Leave wins 53 percent to 48 percent.

June 24 Cameron resigns as prime minister.

July 11 Theresa May is elected leader of the Conservative Party and assumes the role of prime minister. "Brexit means Brexit," she says, but details are scarce.

2017

January 17 Theresa May delivers a speech on Brexit that finally lays out the government's twelve-point plan for exiting the European Union. "What I am proposing cannot mean membership of the Single Market," she says.

January 24 The High Court rules that an act of Parliament is required to trigger Article 50, the formal mechanism by which a nation may leave the EU.

March 13 Parliament votes to give May the authority to trigger Article 50.

March 29 May triggers Article 50. The process, by default, takes two years. Some experts believe that completely disentangling the UK and the EU, and establishing new trade deals and pacts, could take a decade.

April 18 May calls for a snap election, hoping to secure a mandate so that she may approach Brexit negotiations with a stronger hand.

June 8 General Election. Labour, under the leadership of Jeremy Corbyn, makes a strong showing, picking up thirty seats in Parliament. Meanwhile, May's Conservative Party, rather than securing a mandate, loses its majority, resulting in a hung Parliament.

May 7 Pro-Europe centrist Emmanuel Macron wins France's presidential election, soundly defeating the far-right candidate Marine Le Pen, who at one point had advocated for France's exit from the EU—Frexit. After the election, she acknowledges that her Frexit policy proved deadly to her campaign.

June 19 Article 50 negotiations begin.

Bibliography

Books

Arron Banks, *The Bad Boys of Brexit: Tales of Mischief, Mayhem and Guerrilla Warfare in the EU Referendum Campaign.* London: Biteback, 2017.

Owen Bennett, *The Brexit Club: The Inside Story of the Leave Campaign's Shock Victory.* London: Biteback, 2016.

Gary Gibbon, *Breaking Point: The UK Referendum on the EU and its Aftermath.* Haus Publishing, 2016.

Tim Shipman, *All Out War: The Full Story of How Brexit Sank Britain's Political Class.* London: William Collins, 2016.

Periodicals

Anne Applebaum, "Everyone Said Old Europe Was Dying. Sure Doesn't Look Like It Now," *Washington Post*, June 16, 2017. www.washingtonpost.com.

Carole Cadwalladr, "The Great British Brexit Robbery: How Our Democracy Was Hijacked," *Guardian*, May 7, 2017. www.theguardian.com.

Matthew d'Ancona, "Brexit: How a Fringe Idea Took Hold of the Tory Party," *Guardian*, June 15, 2016. www.theguardian.com.

Thomas Frank, "From Rust Belt to Mill Towns: A Tale of Two Voter Revolts," *Guardian*, June 7, 2017. www.theguardian.com.

Joshua Green, "Nigel Farage Goes to Washington," *Bloomberg Businessweek*, December 8, 2016. www.bloomberg.com.

Sarah Lyall, "Will London Fall?" *New York Times*, April 11, 2017. www.nytimes.com.

Sam Knight, "The Man Who Brought You Brexit," *Guardian*, September 29, 3016. www.theguardian.com.

John Micklethwait, "Goodbye to All That," *Bloomberg Businessweek*, June 29, 2016. www.bloomberg.com.

Bill Powell, "How Europe Can Save Itself After Brexit," *Newsweek*, July 2, 2016. www.newsweek.com.

David Runciman, "How the Education Gap Is Tearing Politics Apart," *Guardian*, October 5, 2016. www.theguardian.com.

Zadie Smith, "Fences: A Brexit Diary," *New York Review of Books*, August 18, 2016. www.nybooks.com.

Websites

Brexit (https://www.ft.com/brexit?mhq5j=e3). The landing page for all of the *Financial Times*' Brexit coverage, including an article timeline, podcast, and daily briefing.

Brexit Weekly Briefing (https://www.theguardian.com/politics/eu-referendum). The writers and editors at the UK newspaper the *Guardian* compile a weekly rundown of the latest twists and turns in the Brexit saga.

Center for Economic Performance (http://cep.lse.ac.uk/BREXIT/). This site, which is sponsored by the London School of Economics, features a host of Brexit-focused articles, reports, and videos.

EU Brexit Taskforce (https://ec.europa.eu/info/departments/taskforce-article-50-negotiations-united-kingdom_en). This is the website for the EU taskforce that will conduct Article 50 negotiations with the UK.

Plan for Britain (https://www.planforbritain.gov.uk). This government website provides details and insights into the United Kingdom's plan for exiting the European Union.

Index

E

F

G

H

I

J

K

L

M

N

O

P

R

S

T

U

V

W

X

Y

Z